# CONFESSIONS OF A WICKED FAE

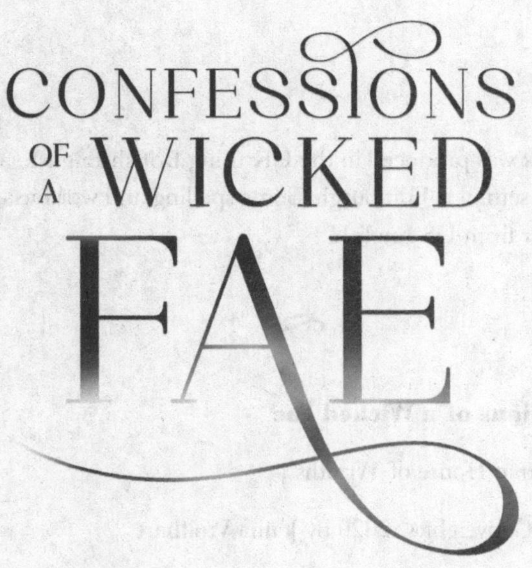

# JENNA WOLFHART

**Confessions of a Wicked Fae**

Book Two in House of Wraiths



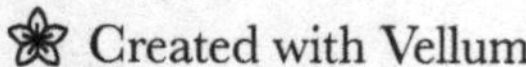 Created with Vellum

# CASTLE WRAITH

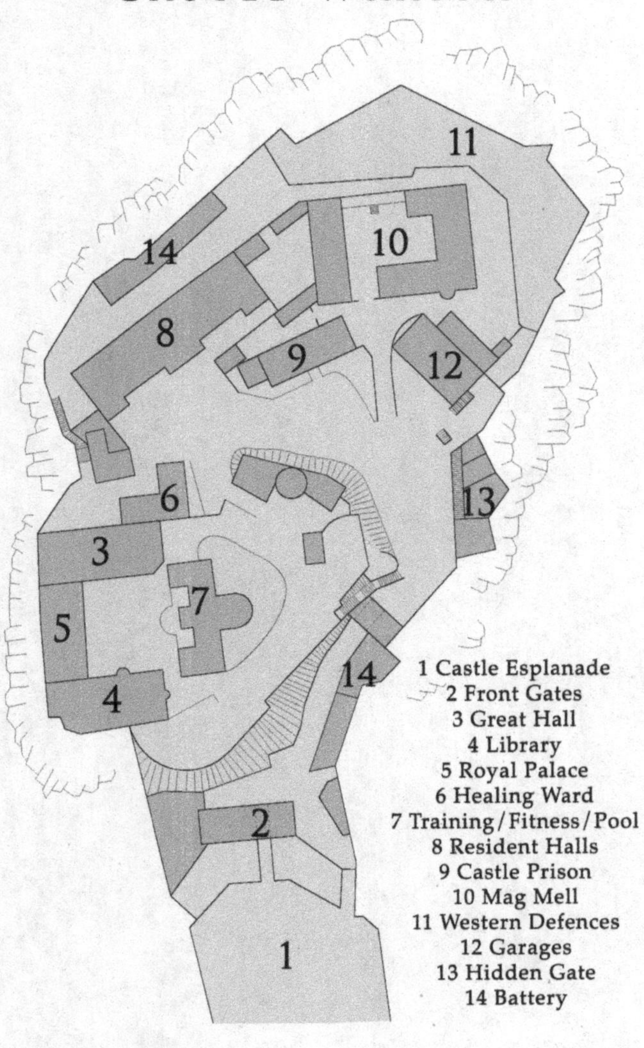

# THE RAVEN COURT

Queen of Faerie
Clark Cavanaugh (The Morrigan)

The King Consort
Balor Beimnech (The Smiter)

## Houses within the United Kingdom

House Beimnech (England)
Led by Queen Clark Cavanaugh

House Futrail (Northern Ireland)
Led by Master Tiarnan Breathnach

House Driscoll (Wales)
Led by Master Rhiannon Rees

~~House Athaira (Scotland)~~
~~Led by Master Athaira Archer~~
Court of Wraiths (Scotland)
Led by King Lugh Tuireann

Master is a unisex title that can refer to both male and female fae leaders. They defer to the Queen.

Solitary fae - a fae who is not a member of the Court and is lacking the full strength of their powers.

The frozen tip of my nose threatened to break off and join the snow-blanketed ground. I stood in the middle of nowhere, burrowing deep into my thick coat and wishing I could turn back time. Northern Faerie was *cold*. Understatement of the century.

"Caer isn't here," I said to Axel, a grumpy-yet-loyal sorcerer, who had been helping me track down the wily druid. We'd followed her through the portal, into the fae realm, across the rolling hills now teeming with life, through the warm summer lands, and up where ice was more common than air itself.

We stood on a frozen field, staring at a stretch of rocky foothills that backed up to a looming mountain covered in ice and crisp white snow.

We'd heard rumours that Caer hid in these hills now, lurking inside a hut with no roof. But there was nothing to see here other than ice. And more ice.

And then a little bit more ice.

"No," the sorcerer grunted. Axel towered over me, and he was built more like a werewolf than a human. He had long hair and a bushy beard, tattoos spiralling across muscular arms that were now hidden beneath his thick coat.

At first, I'd been a little hesitant about asking him for help, but he'd saved Lugh's life once before. If I could trust any sorcerer, it would be him. With the magic of the ley lines running through his veins, he could use the magic in ways that I could not. And he knew how to track anyone down, so long as he had a name in his mind.

Unfortunately, it turned out his magic didn't work as well in Faerie as it did in the mortal realm. We'd been able to track Caer this far, but Axel couldn't pinpoint her exact location. She could be anywhere inside the twenty mile radius in which we stood.

I blew out a breath that fogged before me. "What are you thinking?"

"I'm thinking it's colder than a vampire's teat."

"You're not wrong there." I gazed across the frozen tundra. "Think we should search the mountains? It looks like the perfect place for a druid to hide."

"Thing is, Moira," the sorcerer began, shoving his hands deep into his coat pockets, "it's clear this Caer mate of yours is a wee bit shy."

I snorted. "Caer? *Shy?* That's not even close to being true. She loves blasting people with prophecies."

"Maybe 'shy' is the wrong word," he corrected. "But she sure as hell doesn't want to be found right now. She *could* be in those mountains, but even if she was, she won't let us find her. She's been on the move since we arrived in Faerie."

"You think she knows we're looking for her?" I turned to gaze up at the towering sorcerer. "It's not like her to avoid the chance to give someone a grim, terrifying prophecy that will haunt their every last waking moment. Plus, I brought her a gift."

I held up the box of treats—chocolate covered bugs—and shook it.

Axel shrugged. "I don't know what to tell you.

All I know is she's been evading us all this time, and I'm ready to head back home."

A strange chill suddenly swept down my spine. Stiffening, I cocked my head and focused my enhanced fae hearing on the snow-packed ground behind us. Something snapped, but it was impossible to tell what. Was someone here?

"Caer?" I called out, twisting around to face the empty space behind us.

Axel went rigid, and his hand slipped back into his pockets. I wasn't entirely sure what he hid in there, but I knew it was a weapon of some sort. Every time even something even mildly threatening had happened along our journey together, he'd shoved his hands right back into his pockets again.

Another snap. And then another.

I narrowed my eyes. "I know someone is there. I can hear you. Show yourself."

Three imposing fae whispered out of shadows that had not been there a moment before. I blinked and stepped back, more from surprise than anything else. There weren't any trees to hide behind. There were no rocks. Just miles and miles of snow. The shadows vanished as easily as they'd appeared.

The fae were all dressed in ancient garb.

Leather armor with shields and swords, along with helmets that covered their unruly hair. All female warriors, and all looking very ready for a fight.

"What are you doing here?" The tallest stepped forward, rolling back her shoulders in a classic move meant to intimidate. Didn't really work on me. She might have caught me by surprise, but she'd have nothing on my skill with the blade.

"I'm looking for Caer." I dropped my hand to the hilt of my sword and rubbed my thumb against the soothing gold. "She's a druid, and—"

"The Goddess of Prophecies and Dreams," the fae said, cutting me off. She narrowed her eyes. "Do not merely refer to her as a druid. It's blasphemy."

*Blasphemy?*

I fought the urge to roll my eyes. "Yeah, all right. Sure. The goddess of prophecies and dreams. Have you seen her?"

"No one may see Caer. She is a Goddess. You may offer her your prayers, and then you must go. We know you have been tracking her, and you must stop. Or you will face the wrath of the blade."

Okay, so this was weird. Caer had returned to

Faerie two years ago, seemingly alone. The world here had still been rebuilding itself from a long-ago war, and most fae still preferred the luxuries of the human world to a forgotten land. But some must have followed her here. And they were… worshipping her now?

"Look, I know Caer. We kind of go way back. I just want to talk to her about a prophecy she gave me a long time ago." I curled my fingers around the hilt of my sword. "So I'll ask again. Do you know where I can find her?"

The fae stepped forward and hissed. "Caer will no longer be dispensing prophecies like candies. You will offer your prayers, and a sacrifice if you wish, and you will be deemed worthy or not."

"I'm thinking unworthy," one of the other fae said in a bored voice.

I cut my eyes to Axel. "You happen to have a potion that gets rid of three pesky fae?"

"That would be a negative," he said with a minute shake of his head. "Though I don't think that'll solve our problem if you want to see Caer. Maybe just do the prayer thingy."

"Right." I turned back to the strange armoured fae. "What exactly does the prayer thingy entail?"

The leader pursed her lips and narrowed her eyes. "You do not seem to be taking this very seriously."

"I just don't understand it," I insisted. "Tell me what I have to do, and then I can make an informed decision."

She twisted to glance at her buddies. They both shook their heads. Hmm. Not a great sign.

When she turned back, I swore her eyes flashed with glee. "You must prostrate yourself on the frozen ground and offer your life in service to Caer. If you are worthy, then we will take you to see her."

My eyebrows shot up. "Prostrate myself? You've got to be bloody joking."

Her lips went white as she pressed them tightly together. Right. So, not joking then.

"I'm not really a prostrating kind of person," I mumbled as I glanced back at Axel. He merely gave me a shrug, as if to say, 'How badly do you want to ask Caer about your prophecy?'

My heart thumped. I'd pretty much do anything at this point. As much as it pained me to admit, Caer had the answers that I needed. It had been weeks since I'd seen Lugh, and it felt like a hole had been punched through my heart. Every day, I thought about going back to him, and every day, I had to talk myself out of it. His life was on the line. I would not allow myself the luxury of his company just because I selfishly didn't want to be without him.

Being *with* him would only end in his death.

Our relationship was doomed. Unless Caer knew a way out of it.

I sucked in a deep breath and sank down to my knees. Then before I could talk myself out of it, I fell face forward onto the snow. A second later, hysterical laughter echoed all around me. I jerked up from the ground, narrowing my eyes to see the three fae doubled over, tears running down their faces.

"I didn't think she'd actually do it!" the leader shrieked, pointing at me.

I jumped to my feet and drew my sword. The steel sang as it whistled through the air. Their laughter died on their lips.

"Tell me what the fuck is going on. Now." I growled the words. "I did what you said. Where the hell is Caer?"

"Who knows?" the leader said with a shrug, and then grinned again. "We're not really her worshippers. We're just bored and haven't seen anyone come through here in a long time. We thought it'd be fun…" Her eyes flicked to my sword. "Honestly, it was just for a laugh. No harm, no foul. Right?"

"No harm?" I growled, stalking closer. "No foul? You just made me bloody prostrate myself before you."

"Yeah, you must really, really want to see Caer." She took a step back. "Please put that away. We don't want any trouble."

"If you didn't want any trouble, then you shouldn't have acted like a bunch of bloody wankers," I snapped back.

Axel's strong, warm hand found my arm, and he dragged me back. "They're not worth it."

No, they *weren't* worth it, but the anger rushing through my veins was more than just that. It was sorrow and pain, roiling through me like a snake. Caer had been my only hope for finding a way to break the prophecy. For a moment, I'd felt hope that we'd finally managed to track her down. Instead, I'd gotten pied in the face.

Silently, Axel led me away from the still-laughing trio. We stomped through the snow toward the white-peaked mountains, but took a left at the fork in the path. We were heading back south, down toward the portal, instead of continuing further north where Caer was hiding in the hills. I didn't even try to argue with his choice. I knew it was the right one to make. Caer clearly did not want me to find her, which meant I never would. We'd been searching for her for weeks.

Finally, after what felt like hours of silence, Axel gave a shake of his head. "Well, that didn't really go according to plan."

No, it hadn't. Another understatement of the century. I was practically swimming in them at this point. For the past month, I'd been on the hunt for anything that could give me a cure, anything that could tell me how to reverse the damn prophecy.

My heart ached when I thought of Lugh. I couldn't get his handsome face, his dark eyes, and those midnight blue strands of hair out of my head.

Lugh was my mate, and I still didn't know if I could ever see him again.

2

As soon as I hauled myself out the Lake of the Dragon's Mouth—the portal to Faerie, located deep inside the Devon forests—a strange metallic scent burned my nostrils. Immediately, I was on my feet with my sword in hand, pulling myself up tall, like a bad-ass warrior—though I probably looked more like a drowned rat. My hair clung to my face and rivulets of lake water dripped onto my boots.

"Hello, noble warrior," a high-pitched voice rang out as a small green creature leapt through the air. "It is I, Uisnech!"

I lowered my sword, and a smile tugged at the corners of my lips. Lugh's second-closest advisor and oldest friend stood before me. He was about as tall as my waist with feet twice the size of mine, and he had long, curling ears and a snout that glowed green. I had not been fond of the creature when we'd first met. Hobgoblins were notorious for trickery.

"Uisnech!" My smile widened even more. "I'm sorry I aimed my sword at you. I didn't expect anyone to be here. What are you doing at the Lake of the Dragon's Mouth?" My smile dimmed. "Is everything okay at Castle Wraith?"

*Is everything okay with Lugh?* That was the question I truly wanted to ask, but I couldn't bring myself to say his name aloud. Hell, I could barely think it without wanting to double over from the gut punch it gave me.

His green eyes flickered. "Alas, it is not, my noble friend. That is why I have come all this way. To intercept you before you return to your Raven Court."

The Raven Court was the name that Clark had chosen for her new unified rule over the fae of the world. It had a nice ring to it, even if it was incredibly straightforward. Clark was half-shifter, and she could transform herself into a raven. She was also the Morrigan, one of the most powerful fae to have ever lived.

And she was my queen.

Axel's head crested the waters in the lake

behind me, and he hauled himself onto the grassy shore. Uisnech's eyes narrowed as he glanced suspiciously from the sorcerer to me and then back again.

"Why are you here with this man?" Uisnech asked accusingly. "You are the king's mate."

Even though Clark was Queen of Faerie, Lugh had fashioned himself his own Court called the Court of Wraiths, and he was the king of it. It was meant for outcasts, runaways, former criminals, and those who had no home. He welcomed anyone who had nowhere else to go. At first, Clark hadn't been too sure about the whole thing. The entire point of her reign was to bring all the fae together. For everyone to get along.

But Lugh and his fae just wanted peace, privacy, and the freedom to live how they wanted.

So she'd agreed to give him a trial period. As long as he and his fae did nothing to threaten anyone else, then she would quietly let him continue with his secret Court. No one else was to know about it, however. If the other fae, who had once been members of other Courts, found out, they would likely stage a revolt. Obviously, no one wanted that, least of all Lugh.

"Don't worry, little goblin. I would never get

involved with a fae," Axel grunted. "Too much drama."

"Right back at you, mate," I said before turning to Uisnech. "What's going on? Is…*everyone* okay?"

Uisnech twisted his little green hands together, his expression full of unease, his bushy eyebrows pinched. He glanced from the sorcerer to me, and then back to the sorcerer again.

"You can trust Axel," I said. "He's the one who helped save Lugh's life that night we got attacked in Barrie's Close."

Instantly, Uisnech relaxed. "Ah. Well then. You once said that you would return to Castle Wraith if the king needed you. That is why I am here. He needs you, warrior friend."

I frowned. I might have said something of the sort, but I was pretty sure I'd worded it very differently. Otherwise, I needed to give Past Moira a big kick in the arse. Because while Uisnech was unlike any hobgoblin I'd ever heard of, he wasn't a total anomaly. Hobgoblins took vows very seriously. If I'd once promised him something, I had no choice but to do it. He would bind me to my words.

I sighed and closed my eyes. "Just tell me what's going on, Uisnech."

"There is a new plot," he whispered feverishly, flicking his eyes to the sorcerer, clearly still uncertain about his part in this conversation. "One to steal the king's spear."

He gave me a meaningful look. A flicker of fear went through my gut. I wasn't sure what I had expected him to say…partly, I hadn't truly believed there was even a real threat this time. Uisnech had been trying to get me to return to Edinburgh ever since I'd left. I probably had a hundred texts from him about it.

"You mean the *spear* spear?" I asked around a lump in my throat.

He nodded vigorously.

My palms went slick with sweat. The five-pointed spear. It was a weapon of infinite brutality. I'd wielded it once, and it had shaken me to my very core. It could take on anyone and anything, and it hummed with so much magic that it felt as though it could rip apart an entire world.

If the wrong person got ahold of it, they could do a hell of a lot of damage to anyone they deemed an enemy. They could very well turn it on Lugh himself, or even the Morrigan, my queen.

That was one problem with this whole spear plot, but it wasn't the worst.

There was a second, far greater problem than that. The spear held Lugh's soul.

And if someone stole it and snapped it in half, Lugh would lose the very thing that made him who he was. No longer would he stand tall as the king of the damned. He would transform into a nightmare wraith once again.

And he would become the very thing that could destroy this entire realm.

~

For weeks, I'd been telling myself that nothing could get me to return to Edinburgh. No amount of pleading from anyone, whether that be Uisnech, Saoirse, or Lugh himself —not that he'd done any such thing. Lugh might be many things, but a beggar was not one of them.

And yet, I now found myself packing my things and saying my goodbyes to my queen again. Axel drove us back up to Edinburgh, Uisnech in the back. The drive went by faster than I liked. And soon, I was standing outside of Castle Wraith once again.

The castle was an imposing set of buildings that sat high on the jagged cliffs above Edinburgh.

Two towers squatted on each side, an arresting display of the southern and northern defences. Once, those defences had been manned by soldiers protecting the royal inhabitants within, but no one had tried attacking Castle Wraith for years—until a group of fae loyal to Nemain had tried to take Lugh down.

My dread grew as we drove up Castle Hill and across the cobblestone esplanade. Stomach twisted in knots, I peered through the front windscreen at the imposing gates that grew larger and larger with each moment that passed. Lugh would be on the other side of those metal bars, waiting. I wasn't ready to see him yet.

I wasn't sure I would *ever* feel ready to see him.

The last time he'd stood before me, I had run. As fast as I could. Away from the only love I had ever known. And I'd done it even when I'd seen the pain flickering in his hooded black eyes.

He'd been so hurt that I hadn't heard from him since.

Until Uisnech had shown up at the Lake of the Dragon Mouth, I'd half-convinced myself that Lugh would *never* want to see me again, even if I did find a way to undo the prophecy.

The gates swung wide before us, and Axel inched the car forward until we were on Castle

Wraith grounds. I peered out the window as we passed the towers. The guards nodded to us from their perches above and waved us through. Frowning, I glanced around.

"Where's Lugh?" I hated that I asked, but I couldn't stop myself from voicing the words out loud, either. I'd braced myself for this moment. I'd come here to help him. Plus…I was his fated mate, for fuck's sake. Where the hell was he?

"The king is otherwise preoccupied," Uisnech piped up from the back seat.

I twisted toward him and gave him a sharp look. "Otherwise preoccupied? With what? I came all the way up here from London to help him with this spear thing."

"Yes." Uisnech wrung his hands. "The king has been very busy recently. Much is happening in the Edinburgh supernatural world…"

I scowled as Axel quietly drove the car into the expansive garage at the northern end of the castle. When we'd climbed out and grabbed our bags, Uisnech gave me a strange little grin. "You're going to be excited when you see your room."

I glanced toward the residential building that loomed large in the dark. It was where the fae of the Court of Wraiths slept, lived, and hung out—

for the most part. Last time I'd been here, I'd stayed in the only available room—a tiny, freezing rectangle with dodgy heating on the very top floor.

"It's a nice enough room, Uisnech," I said slowly, "but I have to admit, I haven't missed shivering in bed at night."

"You won't be staying there." He grinned. "You'll be staying close to Lugh."

~

Staying close to Lugh did not mean what I thought it meant. Images had immediately sprung to mind. Me, forced to walk down the stairs every morning and see Lugh's sleep-rumpled hair. Lugh, walking through the hallways topless, his corded muscles begging to be touched.

But Uisnech did not lead me to the Royal Palace like I feared—and half-hoped, if I were being honest. Instead, he took me to the building next door. When he led me inside, he smiled as I gaped at the towering shelves that lined the mahogany walls, the glistening oak tables with tiny green lights hanging above them, and the deep crimson carpet that stretched across polished hardwood floors.

"This is the library," Uisnech said.

"No kidding," I replied.

"Normally, we do not allow guests to stay here. These tomes are priceless, and the information contained within is too valuable to let just anyone near them."

It was all starting to make a bit more sense now. Where Lugh's constant stream of books came from. How he so easily swapped out the stacks on a weekly basis. He was combing through this library, looking for answers to impossible questions.

I wondered if he'd searched these stacks for information about me.

"However, my dear noble warrior," Uisnech said, his voice rising with glee. "You are special. You must stay in these rooms."

I dragged my gaze away from the books to meet the hobgoblin's gleaming eyes. "You want me to sleep in the library?"

It was clearly a level up from the frigid room, but there wasn't a bed in sight.

"I have found you a very special room for your visit this time." Uisnech led me upstairs and pushed open a door. Inside, a large guest room sat empty. A fire flickered in the corner, casting orange hues across a four-poster bed. It was a hell of a lot nicer than the place I'd stayed before.

But I'd been a spy that time. And Lugh had known I was a spy.

Hell, he'd probably given me the coldest room in the castle just for shits and giggles.

Uisnech stopped just inside the door and opened his arms. "What does the noble warrior think?"

I smiled down at him. "You know, as much as I love the nickname, you don't have to call me that."

His eyes flashed. "I know I don't. Which is why I will continue to do so. Now, the room. Are you pleased by the fire?"

I twisted on my heels to gaze around the guest room. A crimson carpet stretched across the hardwood floor, trapping in the soothing warmth of the fireplace.

"It's perfect, Uisnech. Thanks."

"Good." He gave a nod. "Settle in. Get some sleep. Explore the library if you like. The plotting begins first thing in the morning."

Uisnech disappeared through the open door and left me staring after him. Suddenly, I felt very alone, even if I was now in a castle full of fae. I hadn't expected to be led straight to bed and given the goodnight. I'd thought Lugh would be waiting for me. We'd bicker and we'd glare, but at least we'd once again be in the same room.

Instead…he'd avoided seeing me.

With a sigh, I dropped my bag on the bed and decided to give myself a tour of the library, even if no one else would. Maybe I would even be able to find a book about erasing prophecies. Yeah. I nodded to myself. That sounded like a brilliant plan. Squaring my shoulders, I headed back downstairs and began to browse the shelves.

As I walked down the first aisle, I ran my fingers along the spines and drew in a deep breath of musty, bookish air. I imagined the stacks strewn across Lugh's bedroom. His love of the written word had been the first thing that had drawn me to him, and it was impossible to see a book now without remembering the way he made me feel. A hollow ache took the place of my heart. Lugh hadn't been lying. Fate *was* cruel.

"Moira," a voice growled from behind me. I whirled on my feet, heart banging against my ribs. Lugh stood before me, his dark blue hair falling into his eyes, a book tucked under his arm. With a sharp gasp, I stepped back and slammed into the bookshelf. He strode closer, a slight smile playing across his devilish lips. With cheekbones that could rival a Greek God statue and eyes that were as dark as night, he emanated power. I found it impossible to do anything but gape.

"I didn't expect to find you in the library," he said as his piercing gaze roamed across my body.

I hadn't expected to find him here, either. Although I should have. The King of Wraiths practically slept with a book in his hand.

"I, um." I cleared my throat. "I thought I'd take a look around."

A frown tugged at his lips. "You're angry."

A flush of irritation filled my gut. "A bit, yeah. I haven't heard anything from you. At all. No texts. No calls. Not even a damn email."

His hooded eyes darkened. "You were the one who left, Moira. And you made it clear you did not wish to be chased."

I fisted my hands. "And yet you had Uisnech track me down so that you could summon me to your Court again. What, you couldn't come your-self? Even though it's *you* who needs helping?"

Very slowly, as if preserving all of his energy, Lugh slid the book back onto the shelf. "I did not summon you here. It was Uisnech's idea, and I tried to stop him. When I realised he had run off unannounced, I knew where he had gone. I would not turn you away at the gates, even if the very sight of you makes me want to tear this room apart."

My heart thumped. "You should have called me, Lugh."

Narrowing his eyes, he strode closer, power and magic rippling off his body in waves. My own body ached to respond, to arch toward him and give in to the need brewing inside of me. Our mating bond sparked to life, storming through me with an intense magic that filled my ears, my head, and my heart.

I could barely breathe.

"You," he said in a low whisper as he dragged his thumb across my chin, "did not contact me, either. Enjoy the library."

And with that, he turned his back on me and disappeared into the night.

## 3

"Good morning!" Uisnech chirped as he hurried into the guest room, balancing a tray full of…well, pretty much everything. Croissants and scones, buttered toast, black pudding, bowls full of strawberries and kiwi, plus porridge and a steaming plate of bacon and sausage.

I sat up straight, blinking the sleep out of my eyes. "Erm, Uisnech. Is the entire Court coming to my room for breakfast?"

He grinned broadly. "This is all for you. Noble warriors need fuel. Much fuel!"

"Yes. Much fuel." Rolling my eyes, I smiled and climbed out of the bed. Socked feet scuffing along the floor, I grabbed the tray from Uisnech before all the food created a kaleidoscope of mush on the floor. "Thanks, Uisnech. I appreciate you looking after me, but I could have joined everyone in the Great Hall this morning."

"Ah." He twisted away and busied himself with something on the table. I frowned and peered around him. He was just picking up the remote control and putting it right back down again. "Yes, well. You see. Lugh thought it might be best if you dined in your room while you're here at Castle Wraith."

"Oh." I swallowed the lump that suddenly formed in my throat. "He doesn't want to see me."

"It is very painful, you see," Uisnech said quickly, "for him to see you and know that you do not wish to fulfil your bond with him."

I sighed and grabbed a slice of toast, nibbling on the end. "You know that isn't true. It's not that I don't want to. It's that I can't. I've spent every waking moment of my life for the past month trying to find a way to reverse the prophecy."

Uisnech scurried a little closer and dropped his voice to a whisper. "I have an idea for breaking the prophecy."

I widened my eyes. "What?"

"Stay here. Be with Lugh. And simply do not kill him."

Disappointed, I turned back to my toast. For a brief moment, I'd had hope again. "I wish it were as easy as that."

"And why isn't it, my noble friend?"

"Because what if something happens that changes everything?" I pointed out. "What if it's an accident? What if, I don't know, something possesses my mind and makes me do it? There is magic out there that can do that. I've seen it happen before. It's rare, but it exists. Trust me, Uisnech. I've thought of a million different ways it could happen."

He patted my hand. "Such is the same for all of life. There are a million terrible things that can happen to all off us every day. And yet we still keep living, trying and hoping and making our way through this messy mortal realm. That is all you can do, Moira. And it is your choice whether you face it head on or if you run."

I blinked down at the little creature. Had the hobgoblin just waxed poetic about life and happiness? I couldn't help but smile back.

And then a banging on the door interrupted the moment. A short fae poked her head through the door, green hair curtaining a pixie face. "The king wishes for Moira to meet his guard team at half past nine. He reminds her not to be late."

After scarfing down some breakfast—alone—I strapped my sword to my back and headed toward the training room where Lugh's guard team planned to have a pow wow about this mysterious mission. I'd come all the way here from London, and I still had no idea what I'd gotten myself into. All I knew was that someone planned to steal Lugh's spear.

While I appreciated the danger of the situation, I didn't quite understand why they needed me.

When I pushed inside the training room, five pairs of eyes turned my way. Lugh stood in the center of the room with his arms crossed over his chest. Beside him stood my dear friend Saoirse with her unblinking purple eyes and hollow cheeks. Saoirse was half-druid, half-fae, and she could sometimes see the future. Not always. I'd tried asking her time and time again what would happen between me and Lugh, but she couldn't see it herself. She found nothing but murky darkness where we were concerned. That probably wasn't a great sign, to be honest.

Out of everyone who called this castle home, she'd been the only to text.

She met my gaze and smiled. Lugh didn't even flinch.

The other three were warriors I'd met before. Boudica and Warin, the ginger twins who rarely spoke. And Nero, a tall, muscle-corded male about five inches taller than everyone else, save Lugh.

"Hi." I held up a hand and half-smiled, half-winced. The whole room suddenly felt pregnant with awkwardness. Probably because every single fae here knew that Lugh and I were fated mates, and that I'd run the hell away from him when I'd found out. "Uisnech said you needed some help with the…spear thing?" I waved vaguely at the whiteboard propped up beside Saoirse. There was a drawing of Old Town scrawled across it in red marker with a circle around an intersection and the words 'A Knight's End' written next to it.

Immediately, my gaze hyper-focused on the board. I knew that place. It was a pub I'd crashed the night we'd faced off against the enemies in Mary King's Close. The bartender there was human and not a particularly big fan of super-naturals.

I pointed toward the board. "A Knight's End? What's a shitty pub got to do with Lugh's spear?"

"This." Saoirse whipped some kind of long

staff out from behind her back and tapped the end against the whiteboard. My eyebrows shot up, and I pressed my lips together to hold back the amused smile. Where'd she get that thing? "Is the arsehole who wants to steal Lugh's spear."

My brows arched even higher. "Um, I don't think so."

Out of the corner of my eye, I could see Lugh scowl at me. Or maybe I just felt the scowl emanating from his tense body. All I knew was that he was scowling right at me, and I didn't dare look. That scowl always had an unintended consequence. It made my heart beat faster.

Confusion rippled across Saoirse's face. "We've tracked the IP address to this pub. I'm certain the owner is the one behind the scheme."

"Whoa." I held up my hands and strode across the room to peer at the board. "Slow down. What scheme, exactly? What IP address? Catch me up on what's been going on since I've been gone."

"Right." Saoirse turned to the board and tapped her staff against the street markings. "Someone has been seeking out supernaturals for a mission against Lugh. We heard rumors it was happening, and then one of our fae went under-cover, to this very bar, and overheard some people talking about it. Apparently, they put an ad on a notice board there."

I frowned, furrowing my brows. "They put a notice up on a pub board to find supernaturals? Yeah, that doesn't sound dodgy at all."

"Well, here's where it gets weird," she continued. "Some similar inquiries popped up online. They were all over Reddit, Preloved, and Gumtree. A request to meet supernaturals who don't like the fae king that rules on the hill."

Finally, I cut my eyes toward Lugh. His face remained impassive, but his jaw slightly rippled as he clenched his teeth. Lugh had been an enigma when I'd met him. At first, he had seemed hard and cruel and as wicked as Nemain. But I had learned that beneath his cold exterior, he was pretty much a sheep in wolf's clothing. That said, there was one thing he couldn't stand, and that was his authority being questioned.

There was probably some part of his ancient past that still echoed through the very depths of him. He had once been a nightmare wraith, a creature of darkness who fed on fear. But he'd been more than just a wraith. He had been *the* wraith. The king of them. Their commander. He had the power to wield his will over them all.

And that was one very big reason why Lugh

could never lose his soul. If he did, he *really* wouldn't be Lugh anymore.

He would be the commander of a nightmarish army once again.

"And so you somehow tracked the IP address?" I asked, turning my attention back on Saoirse.

She nodded eagerly. "Yep. And it went right back to A Knight's End, where that first flurry of posters showed up. It's the pub owner. It's got to be."

"Maybe it's someone staying in one of the rooms?" I asked, remembering that the pub also had a hotel on top of it.

She shook her head. "Nope. We checked. No one has been staying there for that long. He hasn't had any long-term tenants in years."

"Huh." I crossed my arms and stared harder at the board, as if it would flash the answers to my many questions. Why was a *human* going after Lugh? How did he even know about the spear to begin with? And why did he suddenly want to team up with supernaturals when he'd been so angry about them before?

It boggled the mind.

"There were loads of these ads," Saoirse

continued, turning her attention toward Nero. "How many did you count in the end?"

"Approximately sixty-seven."

I whipped my head toward the warrior. "*Sixty-seven?* I thought you were going to say there were maybe ten."

"Sixty-seven," he repeated. "All saying the same bloody thing. Whoever is intent on getting his hands on Lugh's spear is serious."

I didn't blame him. I wanted to get my hands on Lugh's spear again myself…

Ahem.

"So, then…" I glanced from Nero to Saoirse, and then to the twins, and then finally to Lugh, who still avoided my gaze. "Why don't you just go and do something about it? He's human. It's not like he would stand much of a chance against you. Throw him in the dungeon for a year, and he'll probably get the hint that going after the King of Wraiths is a bloody terrible idea."

"Well, here's the problem." Saoirse winced. "He's not acting alone at this point. He put out so many ads that he's somehow managed to find some takers. Some supernaturals have joined the cause. And they're plotting to steal the spear."

"What if you hide the spear?" I offered. "We could take it down to London and keep it there."

Lugh shook his head. "I need regular contact with it. If I sent it away, the separation would affect me. And I am not leaving my Court here alone. That is not up for discussion."

By 'affect' him, he probably didn't mean that he'd miss the damn thing.

"I thought as long as no one destroyed your spear, then you wouldn't lose your soul," I said.

His jaw clenched. "It's not as simple as that. I am bound to the spear, and the spear is bound to me. That means I need it by my side."

"Right," I said slowly. "So burying it isn't an option. And throwing the human into the dungeons isn't an option." I scanned the room. "But you must have something else in mind. Something that involves some sort of sneak attack. Is that why Uisnech wanted to bring me here?"

Lugh's eyes turned my way as he crossed his arms over his chest. A sharp burst of magic stabbed my gut, forcing me to gasp. It hurt to even look him in the eye, especially after our awkward confrontation in the library the night before. "You spied once before. I want you to spy again."

My eyes widened. "I spied *on you*. And *you knew*

I was spying on you. I hardly think that's a great review of my spying abilities."

"I only knew you were a spy because you were my mate." He shook his head. "You were actually fairly convincing with your sob story about being alone your entire life. About being a solitary fae. If I hadn't felt that mating bond snap between us, if Saoirse hadn't seen you coming…I wouldn't have known what you were, Moira. I wouldn't have known you were here as a spy instead of a fae in need."

I pressed my lips together. "I'm really *not* a good spy. You know I prefer to use my sword. Is there some reason none of the rest of you can do it?"

They all exchanged uneasy glances, and Saoirse cleared her throat. "We have reason to suspect that some of the local vamps are involved. And they know all of us."

Warin twisted my way and gave a nod. "The vamps here in Edinburgh aren't like the ones down south. These still feed on innocent humans, and sometimes kill them. Our team here has stepped in more times than I can count."

"So, you need someone the local vamps won't recognise," I said slowly, and then frowned. "But I was here at the Court only a few weeks ago. I got fake initiated and everything."

A flicker of irritation went through me at the memory. I still hadn't forgotten about that whole Sluagh dungeon thing, even if Lugh had been in those eerie tunnels with me the entire time, unbeknownst to me.

At the time, I'd thought it was a test to determine whether or not I belonged in the Court, how desperate I was to join it.

In reality, Lugh had been playing a prank on a spy.

*Fae.* Sometimes, we were arseholes. Not that I blamed him. I probably would have done far worse than that.

Lugh gave a quick shake of his head. "That means you're recognisable to the fae of this castle, but the vampires have no bloody clue who you are. You weren't here long enough for…"

He trailed off into an awkward silence. Wincing, I shifted on my feet. Saoirse coughed into her hand, and the trio of warriors suddenly seemed intently interested in the hilts of their swords.

I needed to steer the conversation back on to the mission, and fast. Spying on this human was pretty much the last thing I wanted to do, but I'd come all the way to Edinburgh. Plus, Uisnech was counting on me. Might as well get this thing done. The sooner it was over, the sooner I could head home to London.

The sooner I could get away from Lugh and our perilous fate.

I sucked in a deep breath. "Fine. I'll do it. What exactly is the plan?"

Saoirse's expression brightened, and she turned back toward the whiteboard. "Brilliant. What we need you to do is head to A Knight's End and ask the bartender about an ad you saw online. Real casual-like. Get as much info as you can. Try to figure out how many supes have joined his team and when they plan to make a move against Lugh's spear."

"Right." My heart thumped. I could do this. Easy peasy. No big deal. All I had to do was ask a few questions, and then I could head back down to London and go back to my comfort zone of hiding from my dreaded fate with Lugh. *This* wouldn't be the day that I ended up taking his life away from him.

Speaking of the devil, Lugh chose that moment to shoot me a piercing gaze, one that brought a heavy dose of magic along with it. My breath caught, and I almost stumbled back. Tendrils of slick power curled around my body.

My knees trembled. A part of me hated it—I was a strong, badass, capable fae—but another, much deeper, part of myself wanted to rush across the room and launch into his arms.

"You'll go tonight," he said in a low, dangerous voice. "And then Uisnech will escort you back home."

The magic that curled around me vanished into wisps of invisible smoke. A hollow ache took its place, leaving me with nothing more than brutal memories of the moments we had shared. I'd get this done and get out of here, sure, but I'd be leaving a part of me behind once again.

And Lugh didn't even seem to care.

4

Unfortunately, I had to leave my sword at the castle. At first, I voiced—very loudly—my many objections of this. Last time I'd forgone the sword, terrible things had happened. But the team made excellent points. I, Moira Talmhach, was playing a very particular role tonight, and that role was this: I was a rogue fae on the run from the king on the hill. I'd been living anywhere I could find. If I had a weapon, it wouldn't be a fancy golden sword. So a couple of pocketknives were all I had.

I stood on the cobblestone street, staring up at the pub's sign swinging in the brisk wintry wind. The "no occupancy" display was lit up in the window, and every table in the pub was packed. There were a couple of empty stools at the bar itself, manned by a familiar bearded bartender covered in tattoos.

The streets were fairly quiet, though a few passersby strode past me on their way home or to a less-crowded pub. I knew I looked alone and a little lost, but I was anything but. The rest of the team was strategically placed throughout the area, watching from windows or lurking beneath lamp posts, pretending to wait for the next bus. Lugh waited back at the castle, protecting his spear just in case.

With a deep breath, I squared my shoulders and pushed inside. The little bell jangled loudly as I entered the warmth of the packed pub. The bartender glanced up but barely gave me notice as he turned back to the pint he poured from the tap. I minced my way over to the bar and slid on top of a stool.

After a moment, he shot me a quick look. "What'll you have?"

"Just a water, thanks. I'm here to talk to you about your ad."

At that, he stiffened and finally settled his eyes on me. His face remained impassive, but emotion churned in his eyes. Then he flicked his gaze around the room before sliding a coaster across the sticky bar top. "Sure. When it's a wee bit quieter. Why don't you have a drink while you wait? It's on the house."

I opened my mouth to argue, but he was already halfway through pouring me a pint before I could voice my objections. "I'm not really here for a beer—"

"Just take the damn drink," he said in a low growl before wandering away to greet the newest patron at the other end of the bar. With a sigh, I took a sip, and the amber liquid warmed my belly.

I continued to take small sips of my ale as I watched the bartender work. I hadn't brought my phone either, just in case. There was too much incriminating information on it, and if the bloke was doing his due diligence, he'd ask to check it. He'd want to see my call history, my texts. I could have deleted it all, but then my phone history would look suspiciously empty. Better to claim I had no phone at all—I'd been squatting, according to my story. No phone wasn't much of a stretch after that.

He didn't really seem like a mastermind manipulator of supernaturals, though. He just seemed…well, normal, really. As he poured a rum and coke for a woman with salt white hair, I took a quick sniff of the air. I'd always been able to pinpoint supernaturals and their particular magic just by looking at them, but if that managed to escape me somehow, I could definitely scent them.

And this bloke smelled one-hundred percent human.

So why was he putting together a team of supernaturals to take down King Lugh?

The minutes stretched into hours. Slowly, as the clock ticked toward two o'clock, the pub finally began to empty until there was no one left in the room except me and the bartender. He'd brought me a couple more drinks over the course of the night, never saying a word.

He grabbed another glass, took it over to the tap, and filled it with water. Then he rounded the bar and joined me, perching on the stool beside mine. "Here's the water you wanted."

I lifted my brow and took the glass. "Thanks, though your service is pretty terrible. It took about four hours to get this thing."

He gave me a slight smile. "Sorry 'bout that. I just can't talk about this business in front of so many people. They won't get it, and I don't want to scare anyone off. It'd be bad business. Rent isn't cheap in Old Town."

I set the glass beside my half-empty beer.

"Because they're humans, and you're looking for supes."

He winced and flicked his eyes across me. I'd donned a pair of faded blue jeans, a thick flannel shirt with a hole in the sleeve, and a pair of black boots. I kind of looked like a lumberjack. A homeless one.

"I take it you're a supe if you answered the ad, but you sure don't look like one."

"I'll take that as a compliment." I sniffed and lifted my chin, trying my best to play the part of a scorned, angry fae. If I were on the run from Lugh, I probably wouldn't be too fond of supernaturals, either.

"Huh." He grunted, drawing a hand across his beard. "Well, tell me your story, then. Who are you? How'd you find the ad? And why did you answer it?"

I took a long sip of water to give myself time to think. We'd gone over all of this at the castle, but I needed to be careful or I'd set off alarm bells.

"You're human," I replied. "Exactly how much do you know about the supernatural world?"

He snorted. "Far too much if you ask me."

"So you know about how the Court system

works, right?" I asked, shifting on my stool to face him. "You know what being a solitary fae means?"

Understanding dawned in his eyes. "Ah, you're a wee solitary. That explains things. Let me guess. The hill king is trying to force you to join his Court, and you don't want to."

I tried not to register my shock. It was one thing for him to know what a solitary fae was—a fae without a courtly home—and it was another for him to understand that, historically, the royals of the fae courts hadn't wanted any solitary fae out there in the world. They'd wanted full control of everyone.

Things weren't like that anymore, but this human clearly didn't know that.

"He's tried to capture me several times," I explained. "Once, he managed to trap me, along with several others. I escaped but he killed the rest."

Total fabrication, of course. Lugh would never do such a thing, but I had to convince this bloke that I was on his side. That I had good reason to go after Lugh.

The bartender nodded slowly, as if this information didn't phase him one bit. "Sounds about right."

I cocked my head. "What's this about, anyway? Your ad wasn't very specific."

"Specific enough to get you to come here."

"I'll give you that," I said, thinking fast. "But that still doesn't explain why you put out an ad asking for supes. Something about a spear? What spear?"

I figured he would expect that a rogue, on-the-run fae wouldn't know a damn thing about Lugh's spear. And I was right.

"You let us worry about that," he drawled.

"Us?" I glanced around the empty pub. "You mean there's more of you?"

He pressed his lips together and went silent. My heart pounded in my chest, and I dug through the conversation, trying to find something I'd said that had tipped him off. He'd seemed to buy my story, and I'd only asked questions anyone else would have.

"You aren't the first supe to answer the ad," he finally said.

I fought back the urge to exhale in relief.

He continued, "We need more than just one supernatural to pull this off. If we both agree to let you in, you'll be joining a team for the mission."

"I guess that shouldn't surprise me," I said. "That castle is pretty impenetrable."

"We won't be storming the castle." He slid his hand into his pocket and extracted a cell phone. "You seem okay to me, even if you are a wee bit cranky."

Cranky? Me? Never.

I arched a brow. "If you aren't storming the castle, then what are you doing?"

"I can't tell you that," he said quickly. "It's not up to me if you can join."

"Wait." I pressed my palms flat on the sticky bar top and leaned toward the human. "You aren't the one in charge of this whole thing?"

He snorted, shook his head, and grinned. "That's what you thought? I'm flattered, but no. I'm just screening supes for the boss."

Disappointment and irritation battled for dominance inside of me. Bartender Bloke wasn't going to give me the inside scoop after all. He wasn't the one in charge. Someone else was. We should have realised. How could a human wrangle a group of rag tag, angry supernaturals whose powers were far greater than his?

The answer was, he couldn't.

"So who's in charge, then?" I tried.

"Sorry. Can't share that, either." He pushed

up from his stool and walked behind the bar, refilling my pint glass one more time. "I'll tell him about you, but it's up to him what happens next."

"Great," I said dryly. "I love waiting."

"Don't worry," he replied with a wink. "You'll get your revenge on the king on the hill. You're everything he wants in a supe. I just have to ask one more thing, and then you can go."

"What's that?"

"You've been here before, and you pretended like you were human then. You asked for a room but ran the hell out of here after you eavesdropped on some supes. What was that all about?"

Damn. I'd hoped he hadn't remembered.

"I was on the run at the time, just like I am now," I tried. "They were fae, the supes who were in here then. From the sound of their conversation, I thought they were working for Lugh. Hell, I thought they might be trying to track me down."

He gave a slow nod, as if convinced. "All right, that makes sense. Give me your number, and I'll have the bloke call you. He should be in touch soon if he wants to meet."

I rattled off the number and slid off the stool, trying to come up with a way to stall. I'd hoped to find answers here at A Knight's End, but I'd only found more questions. Who was this mysterious supernatural after Lugh? It wasn't Nemain from the sounds of it, but that didn't mean it wasn't someone powerful.

I'd hoped tonight's mission would be the end of things, but I was quickly realising that this was only the beginning.

## 5

"*T*ell me what you've learned," Lugh demanded the instant I stepped foot inside the castle gates. This time, he'd been waiting for me.

I let out a heavy sigh, warming my hands in my flannel. "The human bloke is not *the* bloke. Not that I'm particularly surprised. It never made sense that a human would care much about your spear. Even if he got ahold of it, he'd never be able to wield it."

Lugh's expression darkened as he fell into step beside me. We headed toward the Royal Palace, lit up even at this late hour. My heart tripped. He had waited up for me. "I'm not certain I follow. The human isn't looking for my spear?"

"Oh, he's looking, but he's not the brains

behind the operation. Or the power." I glanced up at him, his sharp profile backlit by the bulbous moon. A part of me ached to reach out and trace the line of his profile, to feel his skin beneath my hands. But I bit my lip, holding myself back. Again. "He's working for someone else. Screening 'applicants' was how he described it. He's had loads of them."

Lugh stopped short. "So, it's true, then. The supernaturals of this city have been answering that bloody ad."

"I'm afraid so," I said quietly. Knowing Lugh, he wouldn't take this well. Despite his urge to seem cruel and harsh, he was anything but. He wanted respect but not fear.

Frowning, Lugh continued the trek toward the Royal Palace. He was silent. I could only imagine the thoughts churning through his mind.

"On a happier note, I think I convinced the bartender that I have sufficient reason for going after you," I chirped. "I'm pretty sure I made it through stage one. I'll find out soon if I made the cut."

Lugh's attention shifted my way. I didn't have to see him to know it. I could feel his power radiating across my skin, beckoning me to come closer. "How, pray tell, did you manage to do that?"

I shrugged. "I told him that we're fated mates and that I'm destined to kill you. Thought I'd go ahead and get my murdering on now and get it out of the way."

Lugh's expression darkened, and he growled, "Moira. If he knows you're my fated mate, he'll never give you a call, regardless of what you say about prophecies. Hell, he'll probably try to use that knowledge to his advantage."

I grinned. "It's so easy to wind you up. I didn't really tell him that, Lugh. I'm not a muppet."

"You could have fooled me," he grumbled.

"What was that?" I asked, elbowing him in the side. "Speak up. I didn't hear you."

He cut his eyes my way. "You heard me just fine, Moira."

"Don't even try to pretend like you don't love me. I—" My smile dimmed. Awkwardly, I cleared my throat as heat filled my cheeks. I cast my gaze away, staring hard at the cobblestones that passed beneath my boots. "I didn't mean it like that. Just ignore me."

"Except I do," he said quietly. He stopped, grabbing my shoulders and turning me to face him. Swallowing hard, I looked up into his hooded inky eyes, wanting nothing other than to get lost inside of them. "I love you. And you love me. Please, let's stop this nonsense."

"You're right," I whispered as tears filled my eyes. My heart hurt so terribly, I swore it would burst. "I do love you. That's why this is so hard, Lugh, but..."

"But the prophecy," he said, growling.

"Yes. But the prophecy."

"Saoirse prophesied that my spear would be the thing to bring back Nemain. And it didn't." He tightened his grip on my shoulders. "Not all prophecies come true."

"She also prophesied that I would show up to your Court and spy on you." I ground my teeth. "*That* came true. I also hate to point it out, but since you brought it up...the cauldron is missing and someone wants to steal your spear again. I'd say Saoirse's prophecy still has a chance of coming true."

Pain flickered in his eyes. "It's almost as though you want the prophecy to be true."

I sucked in a sharp breath and stepped back. "Surely you don't think I want to kill you."

"No, I don't think anything of the sort. I think you want an *excuse* to run away from me, away from this. All your life, you have convinced yourself that you will never find happiness. Not true happiness, not like this. Now that it's standing right in front of you, you're scared."

"I..." Blinking my eyes, I turned away from him, shame and anger churning through my gut. It felt as though I'd been slapped in the face. "I can't have this conversation right now. I'm going back to my room."

"And there you go," he said, calling after me, his voice booming through the empty castle square. "You're running away again, right when things get tough. You're not scared the prophecy will come true, Moira. You're scared it won't."

I didn't turn around. I couldn't. If I did, he'd see the hot tears pouring down my face and the horrible realisation flickering in my eyes. The realisation that he might not be wrong.

~

The next morning, Uisnech appeared as soon as the sun inched into the sky. This time, he did not come bearing gifts. No breakfast platter, no hot, steaming mugs full of caffeine.

"King Lugh wishes to invite you to dine with the rest of the fae. You will no longer be excluded from meals." Uisnech chirped the words and turned to go.

"Wait." I sat up quickly in the bed, my mussed golden hair falling into my eyes. "What made him change his mind?"

"He is fond of the noble warrior," Uisnech said sadly. "As am I."

The hobgoblin bustled out the door, leaving me alone with thoughts I didn't want to face. At least, not before a morning coffee. And I didn't want any sugar or milk to weaken the damn thing. I needed it black, just like my heart.

~

*I* didn't make it very far before I was confronted by my fate once again. Lugh loomed large in the library's front door, the edge of his cloak rippling behind him in the wind. My feet paused on the bottom step, and I wet my lips. After our fight the night before, I wasn't exactly sure what to say to him.

"Morning," I managed, my voice soft. Gripping the wooden banister tight, my fingers pulsed with the canter of my heart.

"Morning, Moira." Lugh cleared his throat, his dark irises flicking back and forth as he searched my eyes. "I came to apologise for what I said to you last night."

My cheeks filled with colour. And, here I was, thinking that *I* was the one who needed to apologise. Because he'd been right, at least partially. "You didn't do anything wrong, Lugh."

He strode across the room and stopped before me. Beneath his cloak, I could see his well-muscled chest straining against the thin material of his shirt. My fingers twitched, desperate to reach out.

"I was angry at the prophecy. Not at you." He took my hand in his and squeezed tight. His touch was hot and electric, and it was all I could do not to jump him right then and there. Clark had been right. Once the mating bond truly kicked in, the magic drawing us closer was next to impossible to ignore. It made my head spin. I no longer even knew what year it was.

"You weren't wrong, though," I whispered, blinking up at him. "I have been running away from you, away from this. For so long, I told myself that I could never find love. Now that it's standing right in front of me, I don't know what to do."

He squeezed my hand again, dropping his forehead to mine. His lips were agonisingly close.

All I had to do was press up onto my toes, and our mouths would collide. I wanted it so terribly that I could hardly think about anything else. Screw the prophecy. We could tackle it together, he and I. We would make sure it never came true.

But then Lugh pulled back, taking the warmth of his touch along with him, and reality crashed down around me once again. Pain flickered around my heart. As much as I wanted to give in, how much worse would it be if I did?

I could not risk his life. *I wouldn't.*

"Did you make any progress in finding your druid?" he asked.

"You mean, Caer?" I blinked and shook my head, confused by the sudden change in conversation. "She is proving to be very wily. It turns out, she doesn't want to be found."

"Hmm." He pursed his lips. "Perhaps another druid will hold the answers."

I frowned. "I already asked Saoirse. As a half-druid, she doesn't have the same access to her power as Caer. She can't find anything."

"Yes, I know." Lugh gave me a sad smile. "I have asked her a few times myself. No, I meant another druid. Another like Caer."

My brow rose. "That would be useful, if we

could actually find one. I was under the impression that druids were rare."

"Rare," he said. "But they do exist."

Hope flickered within me, even though I tried to tamp it down. The past weeks of searching had yielded nothing. I didn't dare hope that Lugh might be right. But the idea had sprung into my mind now, and there was no blocking it out. There *were* other druids out there in the world, ones with the ability to gaze at our fate and find a way to stop the prophecy from happening. All I had to do was find one.

"Ah." A smile stretched across Lugh's face. "There it is. The spark in your eyes. I've missed that stubborn look so much."

I smiled right back. "When we're done stopping these wankers who want to steal your spear, I'm going on a druid hunt."

"See?" He reached out and rubbed his thumb across my lip. Everything within me went hot with longing. "The prophecy won't come true. We'll make certain of it."

He leaned down and brushed his lips against mine. Desire curled in my gut as my eyelids fluttered shut. We stood there like that for a long moment, barely touching, breathing in the scent of one another. It felt as if time itself stood still, holding its breath right along with us.

"Come," Lugh growled as he pulled back and held out an elbow. "I'd like you to join me for breakfast."

That wasn't exactly what I'd hoped he would say, but I was partially relieved it wasn't something more. Because I knew without a doubt, I wouldn't have been able to say no if he'd invited me into his bed.

The Great Hall was pretty empty when we entered through the looming doors. Most of the fae who called this castle home preferred to grab some food quickly from the kitchen for breakfast instead of dining formally in the hall. That was usually reserved for the night-time service, when dinner turned into a lively, entertaining party more often than not.

I had to admit, despite my original reservations about Castle Wraith, I did love their extravagant dinners.

A cluster of fae sat at the table nearest to the door. Saoirse, Warin, and Boudica had gathered here. Between them, they were feasting on crisp bacon, sausages, poached eggs, and half-burnt toast. And they had a vat of baked beans steaming from a silver pot.

My stomach grumbled.

Saoirse's purple eyes brightened when she saw the two of us walking toward them. "Moira! Lugh! Come join us."

She would only ever allow herself to be that casual with the king in this company. Most of the fae were much more deferential to their king. Still, Lugh didn't correct her. We joined them at the table, grabbing plates from the stack.

As we filled our plates, a comfortable silence rose around us. Everyone munched on their breakfast, eyes distant as if pondering the day ahead. Indeed, I couldn't help but ponder myself. We had a spear-stealing plot to stop, and then I had a druid to find.

There wasn't much downtime in the supernatural world.

Just before I opened my mouth to speak, the shrill tone of my cell cut through the silence. Everyone went still, and all eyes were on my phone, where it sat next to my plate.

Swallowing hard, I took a swig of juice and then swiped the phone from the table. I pressed it to my ear, heart hammering hard. "Hello?"

"Am I speaking to the fae who paid a visit to A Knight's End yesterday evening?" a silky voice purred over the line. Instantly, my body went as taut as a telephone pole. Not because of his words —I'd been expecting this—but because I swore I'd heard that voice once before. In the pub. The night I'd run into the gang of supes who had been trying to take Lugh down.

I'd never seen his face, but I'd just assumed he'd gone down during the fight in Mary King's Close. He would have been among the enemy fae we'd blasted with Lugh's spear, or one of the many who had been trapped in the avalanche of falling buildings. But, apparently, he'd gotten out.

Heart thumping, I cleared my throat. "Yeah, that's me. I want to take down the king on the hill."

"Brilliant. I want to meet you before I confirm you're on the team. I'll be at Arthur's Seat at ten this evening. Come alone."

## 6

"I don't like this," Lugh said, pacing back and forth across the training room floor. "We know next to nothing about this fae, and if he was involved in the plot to bring Nemain back to life, there is no limit to what he is capable of."

The whole day had passed like this. Lugh and I would talk about the plan, and he'd end up telling me that he didn't want me to go, even though my spycraft was the whole point of my visit. There had been no more half-kisses or hopeful murmurs about druids who knew the answers to all the questions about the universe. He couldn't shake his unease about the mission.

I shrugged my leather jacket over my shoulders. It was half past nine. We had no more time to waste. "It's about damn time you stopped underestimating me, Lugh. I can take care of myself. You've seen how well I can fight."

"You could be walking straight into a trap. Whoever this fae is…he could know who you are to me."

I met his gaze head on. "Yep, you're right. It *could* be a trap. Maybe he did some research, and he's on to me. But if we don't even *attempt* to make this connection, we might lose our only chance at getting a heads up about the attack they have planned."

He crossed his arms over his chest and growled. "I don't like this."

"Tough luck, mate," I shot back at him. "I'm not going to let some arsehole get his hands on your spear."

I grabbed a twin pair of blades from the training room rack and strapped them around my waist, careful to keep them hidden beneath my leather jacket. I probably wouldn't need to use them, but I wasn't dumb enough to go into this meeting completely unarmed. Arthur's Seat wasn't exactly a remote location. It was very popular with tourists, though perhaps not this late at night. Still, there would be plenty of humans around. Enough to keep the fae from going on attack.

That said, I still wasn't going to risk it.

❧

Arthur's Seat was located about a mile east of the castle, an extinct volcano that rose high above the city. At the top, hikers were rewarded with amazing views of Edinburgh, although the climb wasn't particularly difficult. Legend had it that it was once the location for Camelot, the infamous castle of King Arthur. In truth, the very first fae who entered this realm founded the place as their own. Humans, not understanding the ways of the fae, thought it came from wizards.

After climbing the rolling hills, I glanced around. It was windy up here, and I shivered in my leather jacket. A few humans were standing along the hilltop, gazing at the sparkling city lights below. Only one stood alone, in the distance, with a long dark cloak flapping around a pair of shiny shoes. He was tall and slim with a moustache that squatted like a bushy caterpillar above his lips.

He was fae.

Squaring my shoulders, I crossed the hill to

stand beside him. I kept my hands in my jacket pockets, turning to face the direction he was looking. He was staring right at Castle Wraith.

"Good evening," he said in a silky voice that caused goosebumps to break out along my arms. "My name is Quentin. I am assuming you are Moira."

"Yep," I replied. "I answered an ad that took me to A Knight's End. You're looking for supes."

"Quite right."

I shifted on my feet. "You want to destroy the king on the hill."

"Indeed."

Frowning, I turned to face him. "Well, I'd like to join your team. That's why you called, isn't it?"

He pressed his thin lips together, still refusing to meet my gaze. "I called you here because I wished to meet you. To determine if you are a good match for the team. Tell me, Moira. Why do you wish to fight King Lugh?"

"I'm a solitary fae," I said, repeating my earlier story. "He's been tracking me for years, and I don't want to join his damn Court. He killed some of my friends."

"Yes, so I've heard." He turned to face me then, flicking a pair of ice blue eyes across my face. "Why don't you just leave and go elsewhere? It would be safer for you than this."

I narrowed my eyes. "Because he needs to be destroyed. Even if I make it to safety, he'll just do the same damn thing to someone else."

Quentin pursed his lips, then nodded. "Very well. I'm inclined to add you to the team. We could use a solitary fae such as yourself. In fact, I have the perfect mission for you, if you choose to accept it."

My heart thumped hard. That...had been easier than I'd expected. He was going to take me at my word. Maybe I really was a better spy than I'd thought.

I nodded eagerly. "Brilliant. Count me in. Just tell me what to do, and it's done."

A strange smile pulled at the corners of his lips. "Very well. I need you to get into Castle Wraith and have a meeting with Lugh, preferably this evening, at which point you will set off a Sapphire bomb in his presence."

I blinked at him. "You want me to do what now?"

"I would like for you to use a Sapphire bomb against the Wraith King." He steepled his hands beneath his chin. "Is that a problem for you?"

"No, I guess not." I nibbled on my bottom lip.

"But is that really necessary? Attacking him before the *actual* attack seems counter-productive."

Quentin's gaze hardened. "For someone so intent on destroying the king, you seem suspiciously opposed to my plan."

Shit. I'd done it again. Speaking my mind often came back to bite me in the arse, and I feared I'd really shoved my foot in there this time. My pretend persona would probably find this entire thing hilarious. She'd be eager to throw some Sapphire on Lugh. Anything to see him squirm. Instead, here I was, arguing.

"I want to take him down, that's all. And I don't want to tip him off ahead of time that we're coming after him. If we drug him with Sapphire, he'll know that someone is targeting him. He'll go into defensive mode." Shifting on my feet, I lifted my chin and met Quentin's ice cold gaze, daring him to question me again.

"I appreciate your concern, but I will call the shots on this," he replied. "Lugh already knows a plan is brewing. He will have seen the advertisements."

"Right. I guess that makes sense." I shifted on my feet. "So what exactly is it you want me to do? It's not like I can just waltz into his palace and throw the thing at him."

A strange smile twisted Quentin's lips. "Oh, but you can. You're on the run from him, which means he wants to find you. I propose that you *let* him do just that."

My heart thumped. "You want me to get caught. But—"

"Ah ah." Quentin held up his finger and wagged it in my face. "If you want to prove that you are loyal to this cause, you must do as I ask without question."

"And you want me to get caught." I swallowed hard.

This was really not how I had expected this whole thing to go. For starters, I still had next to no information about the plan, even if I had made it to stage two in the screening process. I'd gotten nothing from the bartender. I'd gotten nothing from this creepy fae. And now I had to pretend to let myself get caught. For...what exactly?

Sapphire might make Lugh's inhibitions drop away, but it wouldn't make him give up his spear. I knew him well enough to know that he would cling on to his soul as hard as he could, no matter how drugged he was. So if that was Quentin's plan, it was a pretty dumb one.

"Get caught." He leaned down and unlocked

his briefcase. As the lid clicked open, Quentin revealed a tiny blue orb that glowed with magic. Even from here, I could feel the pull of the spell, and the desire to give in to my deepest needs. "Set this off in front of Lugh. Once the magic has hit him, you will lure him into showing you his spear. It will be kept in a locked container. Make sure it stays unlocked after he's shown it to you."

I wrinkled my nose. "That's it? You just want me to make sure his spear case is unlocked?"

"The magic of this Sapphire bomb is directly linked to me," he continued as though I hadn't spoken a word. "When it goes off, I will be alerted. That is when my team will know it's time to move in."

"You're going to attack the castle?" I asked, arching my brows.

Instead of answering, he lifted the orb from his briefcase and slid it into my hands. It was warm to the touch and pulsing with life. A part of me itched to drop it now and let it explode all over this wanker. Let him get a taste of his own medicine. Not that breathing in some Sapphire would be any sort of terrible tragedy. I'd been dosed with it once before, along with Lugh.

It had been...intoxicating, to say the very least.

"Never you mind that." The fae straightened,

his long coat rippling around his dark, glistening shoes. "Do we have a deal?"

I swallowed hard, hesitating. This whole thing felt off. None of it made much sense. Surely he didn't believe that this would work? Yes, a solitary fae would be able to get inside the castle and set this thing off. Maybe, she'd be able to get a look at Lugh's spear. But it was highly unlikely she'd stop him from locking the case after, even if Lugh was drugged out of his mind.

Not to mention, how exactly did he plan on getting past the added security at the gates? Ever since the attack last month, Castle Wraith had become even more impenetrable. There were guards everywhere. No one was getting inside unless Lugh wanted them inside, and a little magic drug wasn't going to convince him to open the gates to an enemy hell-bent on stealing his soul.

"Sure," I squeaked. "No problem."

With a wide smile, the fae sent me on my way. I clutched the Sapphire bomb tight against my chest as I hurried toward the castle, my heart thumping. Something wasn't right about this, but I didn't know what. And I had a terrible feeling that when I figured it out, it would be far too late.

## 7

"He wants you to do what?!" Lugh stood in the center of the training room, gawking at me. He wasn't the only one. Saoirse, Boudica, Warin, and Nero wore identical expressions. Even Uisnech looked shocked, and that was saying something. It took a lot to freak out the goblin.

I held up the glowing orb. "He wants me to drug you. After letting you catch me. Tonight."

Saoirse frowned. "He wants you to drug Lugh *inside* of the castle? He doesn't want you to try to draw him out?"

"Yep." I set the orb down on the table, desperate to get rid of the thing. "He thinks that if I drug the king, then I can get him to show me where he keeps his spear, and then leave the case unlocked. He has some magic thingy spell attached to the orb. When it goes off, he'll know."

Lugh pursed his lips. "And then he plans to seize the castle, taking the spear along with it, when I'm otherwise…engaged."

"Seems that way." I shrugged. "Although he didn't confirm his plans to attack the castle, I can't imagine what else he plans to do."

"He didn't want to share more of his plan with you." Warin frowned. "Just in case you blabbed to Lugh, I'm guessing. If you set off the Sapphire, he won't be the only one drugged by it."

I pressed my lips together. I really hadn't thought about that. I'd be hit by it, too.

"Okay," Lugh said, nodding before turning to Saoirse. "Get the extra defences into place. Wake anyone who has experience as a guard. We will fortify the castle and then set this thing off. When he attacks, we will be ready for him."

My eyebrows shot up to my hairline. "So you're going to go along with this?"

"It's the best way to stop him," Lugh said. "He will launch an attack eventually. If we do it when we're ready, we'll have the best chance of defeating him. This is actually a very positive development. You did well tonight, Moira."

I smiled and stood a little straighter.

He gave a few more commands to the crew, and then he led me out of the training room, across the courtyard, and into his palace. Inside, his quarters were just as messy as they'd always been. A new series of books had taken the place of the last ones. Several were open on the coffee table, surrounded by half-empty mugs of tea or coffee.

He held up the glowing orb. "You can wait outside with the door shut. I'll set this off by myself and stay here so that I don't do anything stupid while I'm drugged."

I frowned. "No, that's ridiculous. The Court needs you. I'll set the Sapphire off, and you can go take care of business."

I strode across the room and tried to grab the bomb from his hands, but he held it up in the air over his head, well out of my reach.

Scowling, I glared up at him. "Don't be so stubborn. You know it would be better if I were the one locked up tonight."

He let out a low chuckle. "That's rich coming from you, Moira. I don't think you, of all people, can lecture me on stubbornness."

Scowl deepening, I jumped up to try to grab the Sapphire from his hands. Instead of wrapping my hands around it, my knuckles knocked hard against the glass-like orb. It launched out of Lugh's hands, shattering in the middle of the floor.

We both stared at each other, eyes wide. In an instant, I was rushing toward the door.

Lugh's hand wrapped tightly around my arm as the misty blue gas filled the room. "Neither of us can leave now. We've both been compromised."

He didn't look particularly upset about it. In fact, a wicked glint in his eyes gave him away. I pulled away from him. "You're enjoying this far too much."

"I wasn't, actually. But the drugs are already making me feel a bit odd." He shook his head as his eyes went glassy. "This is one strong dose."

He wasn't lying. Already, I felt a tad unsteady on my feet. The room had begun to spin around me, and Lugh...well, I'd been annoyed at him a second ago, but that seemed silly now. I loved him. He was my mate. There was no reason to be angry.

In fact...

My arm stretched out toward him, my fingers snagging on the top button of his jeans. I didn't really know what I was doing, but I didn't care to think about it too hard. I just moved, giving in to an instinctual desire that I'd tried so hard to bury deep inside me.

Lugh cocked his head, a lopsided grin on his face. "What's this, then?"

"You know what this is," I said, slinking toward him. My fingers slid around his waistband, and then slipped up beneath his shirt. His muscles rippled against my touch, his skin hot beneath my hands.

It was if he were on fire. Hell, the heat in my head made me feel like I was on fire, too.

Maybe we both were.

"Moira," he murmured, watching me with intense, hooded eyes. "I thought you didn't want us to do this."

I tipped back my head to look into his eyes. "Of course I want this. It's practically all I think about. But..."

"But the prophecy," he said with a sigh.

I closed my eyes and shook my head, scattering those dark thoughts away from me and into the bin. "Maybe it's time we forget about the prophecy."

He tucked his knuckles beneath my chin and pressed his hot lips against mine. I groaned against him as my core flickered with need. I'd spent so long pushing him away. Why the hell had I been doing that? He was unlike any male I'd met in my life, and the last thing I wanted to do was lose him because of my fear.

I needed him more than I needed air itself.

As his kiss deepened, I pressed up onto my toes and slid my fingers between the dark strands of his hair. He was wearing far too many clothes. Time to take care of that little problem. Smiling, I pulled back and ripped the soft material over his head, gut sparking from the sight of his well-muscled chest.

"I want you," I whispered, pressing my hands against his abs. "Don't think about the prophecy. Just think about me."

Eyes sparking, he wrapped his hands around my arse and yanked me up into his arms. My thighs wrapped around his hips. I pressed myself closer to him, relishing in how the magic sparked between our bodies.

Distantly, a tinny voice tried to warn me that I wasn't in my right mind, but I pushed it away. Sober Moira needed to chill out. She'd done bugger all to help the situation. A plan to reverse the prophecy was great and all, but it didn't truly matter in the end.

All that mattered was being with Lugh.

Lugh slammed my back against the wall, his hungry mouth caressing my neck. His dark power curled around my body, leaving a trail of sparks in its wake. With a gasp, I ground my core against his, desperate to be rid of the clothes that shielded us from each other.

Lugh pushed away from the wall and carried me into the bedroom. He shoved all the books off the bed, and then tossed me onto the soft mound of pillows. In an instant, he was on top of me, kissing me with such a ferocity that I no longer knew who I was.

Magic pulsed between us as we wrapped ourselves up in each other's arms. Between kisses, we shed our clothes. First, my shirt, tossed onto the floor. Then, my jeans, thrown against a lamp. And then his. As he crawled on top of me, arms and abs rippling, I wet my lips. He looked even better than I'd remembered.

I curled my finger and beckoned him toward me, a sly grin spreading across my face. I'd never felt more emboldened in my life, never more in control of what I was doing. A part of me knew it was the drugs, but it wasn't as though the Sapphire was making me play a part.

It had just removed all the barriers around my

heart. I was finally doing *exactly* what I wanted to do. Fear could no longer control me.

"Lugh," I whispered just as his mouth drifted down my stomach. "I'm sorry."

Lugh paused, glancing up to meet my eyes. "You have nothing to be sorry for, my love."

"I do," I said quickly, swallowing hard, speaking while I still had the courage to do so. "I hurt you. Hell, I hurt both of us. I ran when I should have stayed. You know I love you. More than I've ever loved anyone. And I don't want to run anymore. I want to be here, in this castle, and stay by your side."

A strange expression flickered across his face, his glassy eyes clearing for just a moment. "You're only saying this because of the Sapphire."

"Maybe so," I said. "But I mean it."

"And the prophecy? What about that?"

I reached out toward him, desperate to feel his touch once again. Now that I was speaking, I wished I hadn't said a word. It brought too much clarity to my thoughts. Instead of talking about our fears, I wanted to get lost in his touch.

"Nevermind the prophecy. We'll talk about that later."

My fingernails dug into his skin, and he shuddered.

"The Sapphire might dull my inhibitions, but it doesn't make me forget the past." Shaking his head, he pulled back slightly, frowning down at me.

My heart squeezed tight. After all this, was he truly going to pull away from me? "What are you saying?"

"As much as I want you," he growled, leaning down and nipping my ear, "I will not fuck you when you're drugged out of your mind. I can't forget what you've said. The sober Moira would never want me to take advantage of her like this, and so I won't. I will, however, kiss you until you can't breathe anymore."

It was a promise on his lips, one that made my toes curl. I reached up and wrapped my arms around his neck, pulling him closer. I didn't care about the prophecy. I didn't care what might happen next. I only cared about him.

His lips found my mouth once again, and I sighed with a deep kind of happiness I had never known until now. And he kept his promise. He kissed me until the world drifted away from us both.

## 8

Sunlight poked at my closed eyelids. Groaning, I threw an arm over my face and snuggled deeper into the covers, my back brushing up against...skin. Alarm jolted me awake. I threw off the covers, eyes flying open. Lugh lay beside me in the bed, a peaceful expression on his face.

My heart thumped hard, and my mouth went dry, even as an unrelenting need curled deep within me. The covers barely touched his belly-button, and his whole fantastic well-muscled chest was on display. He looked damn good.

Images flashed through my mind. His hot mouth on my stomach. His tongue teasing the curves between my thighs. An ache built inside of me, and I reached out for him, despite everything within me that told me to stop.

*Dammit, Moira!*

Sucking in a deep breath, I shook my head and tried to remember the night before. The Sapphire still dulled my wits, but it did little to muddy my memories. Lugh and I had set off the Sapphire while the guards waited for the inevitable attack. As the magical drug had rushed through our bloodstream, we'd lost our senses.

And we'd ended up wrapped in each other's arms for the rest of the night.

Lugh cracked open his eyes, his face expressionless. "I see the Sapphire has worn off, so you are making your escape."

Pain lanced through my heart. "I'm not making my escape. I'm just trying to figure out what the hell is going on."

"You know exactly what is going on," he said in a low growl, narrowing his eyes. "You lost your inhibitions and finally gave in to what we both want. And now that your inhibitions are firmly back in place, you want to run from me. Again."

"Lugh." I let out an aggravated sigh. "The prophecy—"

He closed his eyes and pinched the bridge of

his nose. "I don't want to hear anything more about the bloody prophecy."

"Fine." I threw my legs over the side of the bed and padded over to the window so I could peer out at the morning streets. Everything looked normal. There were a few fae wandering through the courtyard, and the front gates in the distance looked intact. No blood painted the cobblestones.

I frowned. "Nothing's happened. Quentin and his army didn't attack."

"No." Lugh sat up, the sheets falling to his hips. "Uisnech came to me with a report last night after you'd fallen asleep. The enemy never showed. We kept the extra guards stationed until sunrise, just in case, and we will be extra vigilant today. But it appears they got cold feet."

My stomach twisted, and I frowned. "Something isn't right. That doesn't make any sense."

Lugh let out a heavy sigh. "Perhaps they saw the extra guards and decided it wasn't worth the effort. They wouldn't have gotten inside, even if they had attacked."

He had a point. But still, I couldn't help but wonder. Quentin had never said they were going to attack. Had this all been some sort of test, meant to see if I would actually set off the bomb?

If so, what came next? Regardless of the attack—or the lack thereof—I knew deep down that this couldn't be over. Nothing in the supernatural world was ever that simple, especially not when it came to power-hungry fae intent on revenge.

~

*B*oudica and Warin wore matching hollow eyes. Fae don't need sleep the way humans do, but we still get tired, particularly if we spend the entire night manning defences, on high-alert for any potential attackers.

"I didn't see a damn thing at the southern defences," Warin said. "I don't think they showed at all."

I glanced from Warin to Boudica, who shook her head. "None at my station either. They were a no-show."

I crossed my arms over my chest and raised my brow at Lugh. "I don't think we should assume they've given up. If he's gone to this much trouble to get his hands on your spear, he'll find another way."

Saoirse cleared her throat. "I agree. No visions have come to me, but I have an uneasy feeling about this."

Lugh nodded. "Fine. But what would you propose we do? Keep the extra guards on the castle defences at all times? We don't have the numbers for that. We can handle that on little sleep but not zero. At this rate, we could manage two more days before the guards start dropping from exhaustion."

"Maybe Quentin was counting on that," I pondered. "He could be waiting until everyone is too tired to fight, and then rush the gates."

"So we need to beat him to the punch," Uisnech said, twisting his little green hands together. "I spy a mission!"

I looked down at the goblin. "What are you suggesting, Uisnech?"

"The Sapphire did not come from nowhere, yes?" He arched his bushy brows. "A sorcerer made it. Who did the sorcerer sell it to?"

Lugh gave a slow nod. "Find the sorcerer who made the drug, and he can lead us to the fae planning the attack. It makes sense."

"We could get the names of all the local dealers from Axel," I said. "And then pay each of them a visit. They might not be willing to tell us anything, though."

Warin curled his hand into a fist. "So we will *make* them willing."

e waited for dark. Sorcerers were not like the vampires or were-wolves of the city. They didn't keep to midnight hours, unless they dealt in illegal potions or spells. Anyone who was hocking Sapphire was doing just that—breaking the law. As intoxicating as the magic was, it was strictly prohibited by both the human and supernatural communities. And it could land the guilty party in jail—human or fae, it didn't matter.

After getting the list of names from Axel, we split into three teams. Turned out there were about six or seven different sorcerers who could be dealing in the dark magic. Boudica and Warin teamed up to take on two names. Uisnech and Saoirse teamed up to take on two more, while Nero stayed at the castle to oversee the protection of the defences. That left me and Lugh as a team. And I was pretty sure everyone had purposefully crafted it that way.

Especially Uisnech, who let out a giggle when he pranced down the street with Saoirse by his side, her long dark hair swinging at her waist. I scowled after the both of them. Traitors.

Lugh dipped his hands beneath his cloak, a smile playing at his lips. "I suppose we're partners, whether we like it or not. The others have seen to that."

Sighing, I glanced up at the towering buildings that scraped against heavy clouds that obscured the moon. "Think they know what happened last night?"

"Uisnech knows." Lugh motioned for me to join him as he took to the cobblestone streets. We passed between two spires of matching cathedrals, their stained-glass windows lit up from inside. "He saw you in my bed when he came by last night to deliver the news. I suspect he gleefully told everyone else."

"Hobgoblins are terrible gossips," I muttered, though I couldn't be mad at the little guy. My fondness for the hobgoblin meant he could pretty much get away with anything, and he probably knew it.

"So," Lugh said, slicing his dark gaze my way. The street lamps swept across his face, highlighting his sharply cut jaw. I reached out, without even realising what I was doing, and brushed my fingers against his skin. He shuddered, but his footsteps never faltered. Instead, he continued with, "What are the two names we have on our list?"

I knew what he was doing. He wouldn't push me away, but he wouldn't welcome me in, either. He'd made his position clear enough. *Fuck the prophecy.* If I wanted the two of us to come together, then *I* had to be the one to say it out loud, not him. The words were on the tip of my tongue. All I had to do was open my mouth, and it would all come spilling out.

Instead, I gripped the paper tight in my hands and turned my gaze on the words. "Two women. Jezebel and Rebekah. One lives—"

"Jezebel hides out in Craigmillar Castle," Lugh said with a nod. "We've had to deal with her before. She has a fondness for illegal magic, particularly of the Sapphire kind."

The paper crumpled in my hand as I gripped it tighter. "So we should start with her."

"Hmm." Lugh frowned. "Trouble is, she doesn't deal with fae."

My heart sank. "So she's a dead end."

"Most likely," Lugh said. "Still, we should do our due diligence and check her out."

This was why Lugh was a better king than I would ever be. Due diligence or not, this felt like a massive waste of time. If I were to pick our next steps, I'd send us hurtling straight on to the next name on our list and write off the trip to Jezebel. But despite how alike Lugh and I were, there were a few key differences between us. For one, he was meticulous. He ticked off his tasks with precision and efficiency. I just liked to barge right on in.

Craigmillar Castle was about an hour's walk through Holyrood Park from Old Town. Instead of taking a car, we depended on our own two feet to get us there. Even at night, it was a lovely walk, taking us through scuffling fields of green, past a glittering pond, and by towering cliffs that cast ominous shadows on the streets below them. We didn't speak as we made the trek, falling into companionable silence. My body felt still for the first time in a very long time, as if I were finally exactly where I needed to be. With a sigh, I edged a little closer to Lugh and tucked my hand into his elbow. With his profile backlit by the nighttime sky, he smiled.

Soon, we spotted Craigmillar Castle looming in the distance. It sat on a large expanse of green with thick trees dotting the landscape around it. It was an old ruin, not in use like Castle Wraith, but the stone structure had been well-preserved over the years. A fortifying courtyard wall formed a square with a tower rising high in the center, roof missing. Once, Mary Queen of Scots had fled to this castle when her lover was killed, only then to plot the murder of her husband.

Now the castle stood silent and still, pregnant with tension. Lugh and I came to a stop in the shadows of a tree on the lawn, staring up at the structure. It was not as large or as well-built as Castle Wraith, but it was still imbued with the same kind of intimidating aura.

"Who the hell comes here to buy magic drugs?" I whispered, shuddering at the sudden chill that swept across my body. I hadn't been cold on our walk—the exercise had kept my blood warm—but now that we were hiding in the dark, I suddenly felt very, very cold.

"People who don't want to get seen," Lugh replied. "No one would suspect that a witch lurked inside, dispensing supernatural concoctions."

I arched a brow. "Witch?"

"That's what she calls herself," he said. "Rumour has it she likes the way the word rolls off the tongue, and it has a greater effect on her human buyers."

"Well, come on then. Time to see the witch." I squared my shoulders. "Let's get this over with so that we can move on to the next name on the list."

With a nod, Lugh set off across the lawn. I strode by his side, enhancing my fae vision to better see in the dark. When we approached the castle, a figure whispered out of the darkness. A woman, clad in a pale white dress, her face painted with red lines. She looked like something straight out of a horror film, and even though I knew what she was, a flicker of unease went through me at the ghoulish sight.

"King Lugh of the Court of Wraiths." She sniffed and levelled her gleaming red eyes on me. "Random, no-name fae. Why are you trespassing on my territory?"

Lugh narrowed his eyes, prickling at her words. "This is not your territory. Last time I checked, this castle belonged to the city of Edinburgh. Not a lone sorcerer with an ego twice the size of her brain."

Her eyes narrowed. "Human designations do not concern me. Supernatural ones do. And as far as the supernatural world is concerned, this castle is mine."

Lugh took a step closer to her, anger rippling

off his body in waves. "As the ruler of this super-natural community, I—"

"Ha!" She held up a hand, cutting him off. "You are no true ruler. You lead your Court in secret, hidden from the Morrigan's eyes."

"All right, we get it. You want to work this castle. Whatever." I placed a warning hand on Lugh's arm before he blabbed that the Morrigan knew about his Court and that she was totally fine with it. "We're not here about that."

She arched a drawn brow. "Then why are you here?"

"We need to ask you about your Sapphire."

She coughed, then laughed, and then laughed even harder. The creepy sound echoed off the looming stone walls. "If you think you are going to break down the inhibitions of *this* fae…" She jerked a thumb at Lugh. "You're going to be sorely disappointed. He has a stick up his arse. Surely a pretty fae like you could find someone more interesting." She arched that brow of hers again. "I would be happy to hook you up with one."

Lugh growled, and every hair on my arm stood on end. The sorcerer's eyes widened, though not in fear. Almost, as though, in under-standing. She choked out another laugh. "Oh my.

You two are mates. I don't know how I missed it at first, but now that I've seen it…"

"You can tell?" I asked, just as Lugh shouted. "Enough!"

The sorcerer pressed her lips together. "I see now why you want that Sapphire."

I tightened my grip on Lugh's arm to keep him from shouting anything else. "Listen, we're not actually looking to buy any from you tonight. There's a rumour going around that a fae is hooked on the stuff. We were hoping to find out who it was, so that we can help him."

The words came out of my mouth, unheeded. I hadn't planned any of this, but I was quickly realising that she wouldn't care one bit that we were in trouble. Hell, she'd probably find the entire thing amusing. If we were going to get her to give up her client list, it would have to be for some other reason than to help us stop an attack.

"Surely you aren't suggesting that I would allow one of my clients to turn into a magic addict," she said, her voice going sharp. "Particularly not a fae. I don't deal with your kind."

"You were ready to sell it to me two seconds ago," I said flatly. "So I think you might deal with them more often than you'd like to admit."

She pursed her lips, regarding me carefully.

"You're observant. I like that. And you stand up to the wraith. I also like that."

Lugh let out another growl of irritation, but we both ignored him. "We just want to know if you've sold to any other fae lately, and if you have, what their names were. Then we'll be on our way and leave your territory in your hands. You won't find us here again."

She sniffed. "Fine. But you might be disappointed when you hear my answer. I've only sold to one fae recently, and he didn't look like the addict type. In fact, I'm fairly certain the Sapphire wasn't meant for him at all."

My heart thumped, ears perking up at her words.

"Tell us his name," Lugh said in a low voice.

"Quentin Something," she said. "He wanted me to meet him at his house, or so he said. It was a flat in Old Town, above a pub called A Knight's End. I assumed it was a front at the time, but I didn't ask. Every fae in the city lives in your castle, right?"

"Right," Lugh growled, twisting toward me. "That's the same pub."

"I thought your team investigated the pub," I whispered, aware that the sorcerer was keenly listening to every word we said. "No long-term tenants."

"He must have obscured the truth somehow," he said. "We asked Kyle to hack the booking server, but he must not be an official guest."

A chill swept down my spine. So Quentin *had* been there the entire time. That meant he could have been watching and listening when I'd popped into the pub that night to question the owner. Had he seen me rendezvous with the team outside in the streets?

Unease churned through me. Pressing my lips together, I looked up to meet Lugh's concerned gaze. "I think he knew. The whole thing, I think it was some kind of trick."

Lugh gave a slow nod. "He must have been there. He might have even followed you back to the castle that night."

"And he called me anyway." I blinked, trying to piece the entire puzzle together. "That's why his team didn't attack that night. That wasn't the plan."

But if that wasn't the plan, then what was? Why give me the Sapphire in the first place? None of it made any sense.

"Excuse me," the sorcerer cut in, her voice

sharp and full of irritation. "I have a business I need to run, but no one is going to approach me if they see me chatting it up with two armed fae. Can you please take your weird conversation elsewhere? I told you what you wanted to know. Now shoo."

## 9

*L*ugh made no move to leave the castle. I could tell that he didn't truly buy Jezebel's story. If I were being honest, neither did I. What were the odds that she just so happened to sell some Sapphire to this Quentin bloke without having a clue what he was up to? Especially when she didn't seem particularly fond of fae herself.

"Just a few more questions before we go," Lugh said, his eyes narrowed in suspicion. "You have always been adamant that you do not sell to fae. What changed?"

She bristled at his words. "Nothing. I *don't* sell to fae."

Jezebel, as far as I could tell, had gotten away

with her dealings only because she kept her clientele very exclusive. She stayed away from fae, avoiding Lugh's interests. And the humans she dealt with knew how to manage confidential transactions.

If she'd started selling to lots of fae, on the other hand, she risked a hell of a lot of eyeballs turning toward her little operation.

That seemed unlikely.

"No offence," I said, "but it's kind of difficult to believe you don't sell to fae when you very blatantly sold to Quentin."

She slid an uneasy glance from me to Lugh. "Look. I can see that you're upset about this whole thing, but it has nothing to do with me."

Lugh cocked his head. "What whole thing?"

"I mean, you're here because he used it against you, right?" She looked back to me again. "That's what he said he wanted it for. Now I know that's partially on me, it's just...well, listen. He promised that if I helped him get your spear, then he'd make sure that I could sell to whoever I wanted, no questions asked. He'd even send me a few customers."

Frowning, I turned to Lugh. That certainly shed some light on the situation. Quentin had effectively promised her full immunity with some added income for a bonus. No wonder she'd agreed to sell some Sapphire to him, especially a potent combo.

Which begged the question... "Do you know anything else that you haven't told us? A small tidbit of info that might be useful?"

She crossed her arms over her chest, lifting her chin. "Maybe I do. Maybe I don't. But since you've gone and ruined my deal with Quentin, what are *you* going to do to help me instead?"

Lugh tensed. He didn't much like demands, particularly coming from someone who had worked with the enemy to take him down. "I will revisit the laws surrounding the sale and purchase of magical drugs. With my council."

Lugh didn't have a damn council. He just had Saoirse and Uisnech. And me, I guessed.

She sniffed at the air. "That isn't good enough, king on the hill, and you know it. I need your promise that you will relax the restrictions you've placed upon my business."

This was getting us nowhere. Lugh would never back down. And Jezebel clearly wouldn't, either. The problem with the magic-originated drugs wasn't Sapphire. It was pretty potent but fairly harmless in most situations. The problem was the stronger drugs, the heroins of the magical world. Not only could they kill, but if gone unchecked, they could kickstart an epidemic due to a strange contagion they could sometimes create.

Jezebel might not care if her drugs wiped out an entire city, but Lugh certainly did.

"I said I'll speak to my council, and that's all I can promise you right now. This kind of decision cannot be made alone."

She sneered. "What kind of king needs the permission from his lessors?"

"The kind of king that doesn't want to see dozens of humans and fae die because you needed to make a few extra quid." Lugh stepped forward, anger rippling off his body in waves.

I swallowed hard. This was clearly not going well.

Slowly, I stepped between them. "Maybe we can come to another agreement."

"No." They both said the word in unison, sharp, like a punch to the gut.

"Ooookay," I said slowly. Clearly, neither of them were going to back down.

Softly, I placed a hand on Lugh's arm and

tugged on his sleeve. "Hey. Can I talk to you for a moment over there?"

Lugh narrowed his eyes, his jaw rippling, but he gave a nod and followed me a short distance across the lawn, just far enough away so that the sorcerer couldn't overhear our conversation.

"You're going to have to agree to relax a bit with the restrictions," I said in a whisper. "Trust me. I know what stubborn looks like, and it's that woman right there."

He scowled. "I can't do that, and you know it. There are too many magical drugs out there that can kill. They're like poison. I've never bothered with Jezebel much because she's stuck to Sapphire, which is harmless. But if she starts dealing the harder stuff, she'll have to be stopped."

"I get that Lugh, but she has information about your—"

"What's that?" Lugh asked darkly, pointing in the direction of the sorcerer. I glanced over my shoulder and sucked in a sharp breath of air. The sorcerer had vanished. Of course she had. In her place stood about two dozen vampires. In the heavy darkness, I couldn't see their faces, but I could sense them all the same.

Lugh's words rang in my ears. The vampires

of Edinburgh were nothing like those of London. Down south, the fae had made an alliance with the vamps. They were organised, calm, and...well, *caring* wasn't the right word, but they had some semblance of morality. They didn't kill humans.

These vamps did.

And, if I were a betting kind of bird, I'd put a hell of a lot of money down on them being here just for us.

Suddenly, a figure in white rushed past us. Jezebel's face was as pale as her dress, and her hands were shaking. "Run!"

Yeah, that wasn't ominous *at all*.

"Draw your weapon, Moira," Lugh said quietly, pulling a spear from the sheathe strapped to his back. It wasn't his five-pointed weapon, but it looked pretty formidable all the same. It had a long wooden staff that led to a glistening silver point that looked sharp enough to cut through steel.

I drew my sword. In the distance, the vampires roared.

They rushed us. Twenty, or more, vampires raced across the lawn. Their voices shot into the night sky in unison, terrifying cries of pure rage. Heart hammering, I squeezed the hilt of my sword and bent my legs, bouncing on the balls of my feet.

A slight current of excitement went through me. It had been far too long since I'd truly fought.

The first vampire reached me, and I swung hard at his head. Moving with impossible speed, he rushed to the side. My sword found air, whistling through the night. With another swing, the blade connected with his gut. It sliced straight through his abdomen, and black blood spilled on the pristine grass. I yanked my sword out of his belly and watched him tumble to his death.

Gritting my teeth, I moved to the next vamp, only to find two more instead. They launched toward me with sharp, talon-like nails outstretched. I ducked down low. They flew past me, screeching. Before they could regain their footing, I sliced through one, grabbed a dagger from beneath my jacket, and threw it at the second. It landed with a *thunk* in the vamp's head.

They both fell hard.

Beside me, I could hear Lugh fighting just as hard. His spear sank into vamp after vamp after vamp. I whirled toward the next enemy. Three more vamps loomed large.

They were on me before I could even hold up my sword. Their bodies collided with mine, and my sword flew across the lawn. My back hit the ground hard, my teeth knocking together. The vampires screeched, their sharp claws scratching at my skin.

I screamed into their faces, throwing my body left and right to knock them to the ground. One grabbed my hand and pressed it against the grass. Its eyes were bright red, its teeth elongated. It looked like a wild animal, nothing like the vampires I'd met in London.

With a deep breath, I steeled myself and slammed my forehead against the vampire's. It screeched and fell back, giving me time to slam my fist into the nose of the second. Bone crunched beneath my knuckles. That only left one.

Before I could launch my attack, the vamp leaned down and sank its teeth into my skin. A sharp, stabbing pain lanced through my neck, and I screamed.

But then its weight vanished off my chest. I scrabbled back, my eyes wide as Lugh shoved his spear through the vampire's head. Black blood spurted out, drenching my shirt. It stank of iron and salt and a strange kind of mildew that made bile rise in my throat.

In the name of the Morrigan, these things were as bad as the Sluagh.

"You okay?" Lugh asked, huffing as he tossed the dead vampire onto a pile just behind him.

I stared up at him, my heart still racing. "I think so." Reaching up, my hand smeared against the blood on my neck. "It bit me."

Normally, I wouldn't refer to a vampire as an *it*, but in this case, the title seemed appropriate. These things were like rabid animals. They'd lost any sort of humanity they'd ever had.

Lugh reached out a hand, and I took it. His strong fingers curled around me, shooting warmth into my chilly body. He pulled me to my feet and wrapped his arms around me. Sighing, I leaned into him and closed my eyes. The attack hadn't been anything worse than I had faced before, but I still felt relief at being in his arms.

Suddenly, sharp nails dug into my arms and ripped me out of Lugh's embrace. Eyes wide, I yanked against the grip, panic shooting through me when I saw another swarm of vampires surrounding Lugh.

Several more had grabbed ahold of me, and it took all of my enhanced fae strength to drag myself away from them. My sword glistened in the distance, the light of the moon dancing along the blade. It was halfway across the lawn. Too far for me to make. I danced from side to side, dodging the blows of the vampires. From behind me, I heard Lugh roar.

My heart tripped in my chest, and I risked a glance behind me to make certain that he was okay. The vampires had managed to grab his spear, and one mangy-haired enemy had dug the sharp end into Lugh's shoulder. Blood poured from the wound, splashing onto Lugh's dark shirt.

I jolted, forgetting about the attackers now surrounding me. I had to get to Lugh. I had to knock that vampire away from him. Despite the prophecy, a real, deep fear went through my gut. Lugh was surrounded. He didn't have his weapon. What if he died here tonight?

Tears burned in my eyes. With a roar, I sprang toward him, my feet pounding hard against the carpet of grass. I reached him within an instant and slammed my fist into the vampire's head. The creature stumbled back, letting go of the spear. It was just enough of a break in the fight for me to grab the end of the spear and yank it out of Lugh's skin.

Another enemy loomed over Lugh's shoulder. I curled my hand around the shaft and shoved the spear's end into the vampire's eye. Blood spurted into my face.

I let go of the shaft, stumbling back as I wiped

the stinging goo out of my vision. Another bony hand grabbed me again. And then another. I couldn't see them, but I could certainly hear them. It was a chorus of screams and gleeful cries of rage. The sound rose around me like thunder, complete with the pounding drums in the form of charging feet.

Something heavy slammed into my body once again, and I fell back onto the grass. My head hit the ground. Now I couldn't hear. Hell, I could barely think. There were so many of them. They squatted on my chest. Sharp stabs went through my neck once again, and all the life felt as if it were flowing right out of me.

Distantly, I understood exactly what was happening. We'd been swarmed. By dozens upon dozens of them. They were feeding on me. Hungry, rabid, desperate for my blood. They would drink me dry. Too wild to comprehend the need to stop, they would feed until there was nothing left of me but the timid pulsing of a heart that had no blood to keep it going any longer.

I tried to fight them off, but my body was far too weak. They'd already drank so much of me. The world seemed to tip to the side, and a strange light flickered in a distant corner of my mind. I was leaving the world. It was slipping away from me.

I was going to die here.

The vampires were going to make sure I didn't survive.

And I would never again see my mate.

## 10

I pried open my eyes. Everything hurt. My lungs, my skin, my very bones. I felt as though I'd been smashed to bits by a lorry, ten times over, and then burnt to a crisp. Needless to say, those vampires had done a number on me.

Lugh's face was the first thing I saw. He leaned over me, his dark hair falling into his eyes. I reached up and traced my finger along his strong jaw, wincing when a new wave of pain crashed into every single one of my bones.

"Ouch," I whispered, my throat raw. "What happened?"

"The vampires. There were at least a hundred of them."

Groaning, I tried to make sense of it. We'd been surrounded. I'd fallen prey to their fangs.

Truly, I should have been dead. "How...how did we survive?"

"When we first got to Craigmillar Castle, I sent out an alert to the rest of the team. Something felt off, particularly with that sorcerer who calls herself a witch." He let out a low growl. "The team showed up just in time to fight the vamps. There were enough of us to scare them off, and we got you back to the healers in time to save your life."

"Ah." I sighed and sank lower into the cloud-like pillows. "So I was useless."

"There were too many of them for us to take on alone." His eyes narrowed. "I will make them pay for what they did to you. I will rain down fire from the skies. I will—"

"Lugh," I said hoarsely, pressing a finger to his lips. "Don't become all nightmare wraith on me now. I'm okay. See?"

I tried to push up from the mound of pillows behind my head. But as soon as I was barely forty-five degrees upright, exhaustion swept over me. I fell back onto the pillows, puffing.

"You are *not* all right," he said in a growl. "They have gone too far this time. The vampires of this city grow too strong."

"Ask Clark to send help. The Raven Court has

plenty of warriors willing to fight some out-of-control vamps, especially ones willing to team up with a fae trying to take down this city." I gave him a faint smile, knowing his answer before he spoke it.

His jaw flickered as he ground his teeth. "I will not ask your queen for help."

It was a familiar argument by this point. Lugh was convinced that asking for Clark's help would be demonstrating a weakness he couldn't afford to show. As king, he believed that he and he alone should take care of his people, of his city. In truth, that might have been the way of the world once, but it wasn't anymore. Clark would help. She wouldn't demand fealty. But Lugh didn't know how to reconcile her modern rule with his ancient mind.

"At least we got a location for the spear guy," I said, wincing again. Even talking hurt.

"If Jezebel was even speaking the truth," he said.

"She was," I replied. "She ran when the vamps showed up. Pretty sure she had nothing to do with that attack. They probably followed us to the castle from Old Town."

His expression softened as I huffed out the last few words. "You shouldn't worry about this right now. After what you've been through, you need to rest. We'll take care of the situation. The team and I are going to A Knight's End to finish this once and for all."

"Oh no you don't." I tried to push up once again, gritting my teeth until my back was steady against the wooden headboard. "You can't go rushing off to confront this guy without me."

"It needs to be done. Now. As you said, he knew you were on my side the entire time. Your prior hunch was right. He knew you would warn me and that we would increase our guards. Now he's biding his time. We cannot allow him to have any more of it."

"You have fae skilled in healing," I said, glancing at the open door. "They can get me back into fighting shape in no time."

"Not fast enough. We need to go. Now."

I pressed my lips together. I recognised the expression on his face well enough. I'd made it a million times myself. He would go confront Quentin at A Knight's End regardless of what I said. He was too stubborn to back down.

"At least tell me the plan," I said. "You know, since I have to sit on the sidelines. I need to live vicariously through you."

He hesitated for a moment, but then sank

into the chair beside the bed. "I'm only taking a small team with me, so that we can continue to have the increased guard numbers on the castle walls."

I nodded. That made sense.

"Uisnech and Saoirse will stay behind. They aren't fully trained fighters, and I shouldn't have dragged them into the field last night. Instead, I'm taking the warrior twins and a few others. We have a solid team formed."

"And what will you do?" I asked. "If he sees you coming, he'll probably bolt. Judging from his past actions, I don't think he wants hand-to-hand combat. He likes his sneak attacks."

Lugh nodded in agreement. "He is a schemer, not a fighter. We don't plan to barge in through the front door. We'll find a way to sneak in through the back. The element of surprise will be important for this one."

"Okay," I said, trying on a smile. It hurt to even do that. My mind whirred as I tried to find another question I could ask. I didn't want him to leave, not without me.

He smiled back, the light reaching his eyes. Slowly, he stood to go but didn't turn until he'd dropped a soothing kiss on my forehead. Even at the slightest of touches, the magic curled around our bodies, beckoning us to remain as close as we were.

"You should get some rest," he said softly, fingers drifting down to my neck, to where the vampires had sucked out my life-force. "When I get back, all of this will be over and then..."

And then what? I didn't know anymore. I would have no more excuses for why I had to stay. I'd have to return south to my Court and say goodbye to my mate once again. Lugh seemed to read my mind. He gave me a sad smile and crossed the room, heading for the door.

"Lugh," I said, my voice going sharp as I called after him. Heartbeat pounding in my ears, I lifted a hand, beckoning him to return to my side. He did, striding back over and taking my hand, but he didn't sit. He'd made up his mind, and there was no turning back from it now. I could try to crawl out of this bed and go after him, but I knew as well as he did that I would probably pass out from the pain before I even made it out of the castle.

"Moira." He lifted my fingers to his lips and kissed me fiercely. "I know what you're going to say—"

"Don't do anything stupid," I hissed, tears filling my eyes. "I have a bad feeling about this."

His lips quirked up in the corners. "Out of everyone, I thought *you* would be the last to forget the prophecy. You're the one who is fated to kill me, yes? So that means I can't die in this fight tonight."

I opened my mouth to argue, and he laughed.

"This isn't funny," I said.

"Isn't it?" He grinned broadly. "If you're convinced the prophecy will come true, then you have nothing to worry about. Like you always tell me, I can take care of myself."

Frowning, I tried to come up with another argument, but he had a point. Damn him. "I mean, maybe I've been wrong. Maybe all this time I've worried for nothing. We don't know what you're walking into, Lugh…"

He leaned down and tucked a finger beneath my chin, his eyes flickering as they stared deeply into mine. "Either you believe it will come true, or you don't." For a moment, he didn't speak, considering his next words. "And if you don't, then perhaps you should consider what you truly wish your future to be."

Lugh turned and strode out of the healing ward room, leaving me frowning after him. My heart thumped hard as my mind whirred from his words. Uneasy, I wanted to call after him, though

I knew nothing I said would stop him from heading out into the night. Hell, I wanted to jump out of the bed and run after him, mind-numbing pain and all.

Maybe I really had been wrong. It wouldn't be the first time in my life. All this time, I'd been focusing on my fear of what could happen, but even druids couldn't predict the future with absolute certainty. My answer had been to run away from it all, to flee instead of facing the possibility head on.

But maybe…I stared after Lugh, my heart tripping.

Maybe I didn't need to run.

fter Lugh vanished, the healing fae stopped by my room again and applied another dose of magic to my aching body. I fell asleep almost instantly, knocked out from the strength of her power. When I came to moments or hours later, I found myself alone in my room, wounds barely flickering with pain.

Squinting against the overhead fluorescent lights, I pushed up and snatched my phone from the bedside table. The display said it was well past midnight. Lugh hadn't come back to my room, at least not that I was aware of. Suddenly, my phone dinged with a new text message alert.

My eyes flicked across the screen.

*They're going for the spear. Now.*

My heart skipped a beat, and instantly, I was on my feet. I didn't recognise the number, so it was likely a message from Nero or Warin, whose numbers I didn't have programmed into my phone. Frowning, I shot off a quick message in response.

*Who is this? Where are you? Where's Lugh?*

No response.

Gritting my teeth, I shoved my phone into my back pocket and slid my feet into my thick boots that had been left by the door. Pain flickered through me, a reminder that I still wasn't fully healed. But I couldn't huddle in this bed when Lugh's spear—and soul—could be moments away from being stolen.

I knew where Lugh kept his spear hidden. While the others were out of the castle doing who knew what, I would stand guard against any attackers. And this time, I wouldn't have to hide my sword.

Jogging out of the healing ward, I passed one of the nurses who had been tending to my wounds. She frowned and stood in the center of the corridor, blocking my escape. Crossing her arms, she shook her head. "I'm under strict orders to keep you confined here until you've fully recovered, Moira. King's commands."

"The king is in trouble," I said, my breath huffing as I slid to a stop in front of her. "If I don't go now, Castle Wraith could fall."

Another understatement of the century. The castle wouldn't just fall if Lugh lost his soul. The entire realm could descend into chaos. If he called the nightmare wraiths out of Faerie, humans and fae alike would spend the rest of their lives terrorised by fear. Those who survived, anyway.

The nurse's eyes widened, but she didn't budge. "How do I know you're telling the truth?"

"You just have to trust me. I'm the king's mate."

Her eyes flickered with doubt, but she stepped aside. Giving her a smile of thanks, I rushed past her and out of the building. My feet pounded on the uneven cobblestones as I twisted around the corner and aimed for the Royal Palace that loomed large in the darkness. No lights were on inside this night. Lugh still hadn't returned from his mission.

I tried not to jump to conclusions about what that might mean.

When I pushed inside the building, silence and darkness greeted me like familiar enemies that lurked in the night. My footsteps were loud on the hardwood, but my heartbeat drowned them out. Palms slick with sweat, I made a detour into Lugh's quarters and grabbed two swords from his personal collection, trying my best not to knock over the towering stacks of books strewn across the room.

Armed and ready, I minced back into the corridor and found the hidden wall. It groaned as it opened before me, revealing a pitch black tunnel. I wet my lips, focusing on my enhanced fae hearing. In the distance, I heard the drip of water splatting onto the floor, but nothing else. No sign that anyone lurked in these tunnels, ready for a fight.

I pressed inside, fully closing the door behind me and enhancing my eyesight. The floor came into view before me, but only enough for me to see where I was going. Slowly, I crept around the bend and entered the secret room that Lugh kept hidden from the rest of the world. Inside, there was a desk, a bed, and his gleaming golden case where his spear sat, safe and sound.

Immediately, I could feel the hum of power in my bones, emanating from the weapon. I ached to reach out and touch it, to feel its golden shaft between my fingers. When I'd first seen the spear, I hadn't understood the pull I felt, I hadn't understood how it seemed to call to my very bones. But now I did. Lugh was my mate, and his soul was encased in the spear.

It meant I would always feel an inexplicable connection to the weapon, as though it were just as much a part of me as it was a part of Lugh.

With a deep breath, I turned my back on the spear and strapped one sword to my back, holding the other tight in my hands. I would stand here on watch for as long as necessary.

It didn't take long for something to happen.

Something flickered in front of me, almost as though the very shadows themselves shifted in the darkness. Frowning, I tightened my grip on my sword and squinted at the flicker. Maybe I was just imagining things. Down here in the dark with my heartbeat banging in my ears, it was easy to start to think the very walls themselves were closing in.

But no…there, it happened again. The shadows pulsed. They shifted. They became a tall, rippling form that solidified with every beat that passed.

Gasping, I took a step back, terror charging through me.

Blinking, I tried not to scream. It wasn't one

form at all. The floor dropped out from beneath me, and it was all I could do to stay steady on my feet. It was two forms. A tall, muscular male fae—Quentin—and a terror-eyed hobgoblin. The fae held Uisnech tight in his grip, the end of a very sharp dagger pointing right at the hobgoblin's green head.

"Don't move," the fae warned in a deep voice as I lifted my sword higher in the air. "If you even so much as flinch toward me or in the direction of that door there, I will kill this hobgoblin."

Gritting my teeth, I held my ground. "What the hell are you doing here?"

He smiled. "Coming to meet you, of course. I am glad to see that you answered my text as I suspected you would. Some fae are so predictable."

"The text message." I narrowed my eyes. "So that was you."

"Oh, yes." His arm tightened around Uisnech's neck. The hobgoblin merely stared at me with his big yellow eyes, his lips pressed together. The poor thing looked like he might die from fright.

"I'll admit, the plan did not go exactly according to…well, plan. But it was close enough." He continued to smile. "Lugh is gone.

You are here. And now, you are going to give me that spear."

I snorted, scarcely believing my ears. "You are joking, right? I would never hand the spear over to you. You'll have to kill me first."

The smile dropped instantly, quickly replaced by a spine-chilling, dead-eyed stare. "You *will* give me the weapon. Or you forfeit the goblin's life."

Fuck. I flicked my eyes to Uisnech's face. Staring deep into my soul, he gave a minuscule shake of his head. He didn't want me to go along with this. The poor creature was ready to sacrifice his life in order to protect Lugh's spear. Hell, I was willing to make that kind of sacrifice, too. But it wasn't *my* life on the line. It was Uisnech's. Horror churned in my gut as I dragged up my gaze to focus on where the sharp point stuck into the goblin's skin.

"Leave the hobgoblin out of this," I hissed. "If you kill him, you'll accomplish nothing. *I'm* the one guarding the spear. "

"I have no desire to fight you," the fae said. "Just hand over the spear. I won't ask you again. In fact, I will give you sixty seconds to make your decision. If the spear isn't in my hands at the end of those sixty seconds…well, then you will have a funeral on your hands." He lowered his voice and shifted on his feet. "The hobgoblin's funeral, just to be clear."

"Yeah, I got that, thanks." I rolled my eyes, refusing to let him see the terror churning through me. The seconds were flying by as if time itself had been doused in a vat of Iron Bru. Uisnech had closed his eyes, resigning himself to his fate. I stared at the little creature. My heart raced; my mouth went dry.

Sucking in a sharp breath, I let out a guttural scream. "Dammit!"

I just couldn't do it. Regardless of what it meant, I could not stand here and let Uisnech die. I couldn't "sacrifice him for the greater good" or whatever other kind of nonsense people told themselves so that they could sleep at night after making terrible, life-altering decisions.

Unshed tears burned my eyes as I whirled toward the spear and unlocked the case. A sharp gasp rang out in the tunnelled room. "No, my noble warrior. You cannot do this."

"I have to. I cannot let him kill you," I said through gritted teeth. "Just trust me, Uisnech."

Quentin might get his hands on the spear, but I wouldn't let him get out of this room with it. Not alive. I lowered my sword to the ground and backed away from the open case, gesturing for him to approach it.

"The spear is yours," I said quietly, my hands curled into half-fists by my sides, ready to reach up and grab my second sword the moment he made his move. "Let go of the goblin and take it."

Quentin's thin lips curled up into a smile. He let go of Uisnech and strode toward the case. Quickly, I rushed to Uisnech's side and pushed him behind me, pulling the sword out of the sheath at my back just as Quentin pulled the spear from its case.

The gold gleamed and flickered in the darkness, the magic inside of it roiling with dread, as if it knew it was now in the hands of the enemy.

"You may have gotten your prize," I said in a low voice, twisting my palms around the golden hilt, "but you won't leave here with it."

The fae chuckled, darting to the side just as I swung my blade at his head. The steel whistled as it missed contact. "Unfortunately for you, you are very, very wrong."

Shadows flickered around him, engulfing his entire body until it was completely obscured from view. Growling, I rushed toward him, my sword raised. I swung hard at where he stood, but my blade only whistled when it once again made no contact.

The shadows cleared in an instant. I stepped back, my heart pounding. Quentin no longer stood before me. He had vanished.

And he'd taken the spear.

## 12

It was my turn to wait at the gates. When Lugh returned almost two hours later, I was chilled to the bone. In more ways than one. I'd been half-afraid I'd never see him again. Quentin took the spear for a reason. The most likely was that he planned to use the powerful magic contained within to bring someone back from the dead.

That meant breaking the spear in half. That meant Lugh's soul drifting away into the darkness. That meant Lugh would no longer be himself. He'd be a wraith.

But I'd also been trying to come up with an explanation as to how and why I'd let the enemy take his spear. It all came back to the same answer every damn time.

I should have done more. I shouldn't have let it happen. I should have been faster, smarter, stronger.

Uisnech, of course, was beside himself. He ranted and waved his little fists, angry that I'd saved his life. I was no longer his noble warrior to which he would follow until the end of times. Noble warriors didn't bring on the end of the world. Noble warriors didn't allow the enemy to steal the most important object on the planet.

When Lugh finally strode through the gates, he looked as tired as my soul felt. Dark circles lined his eyes, and blood splattered his cheek. He moved as if a heavy barbell sat on his shoulders, slow and unsteady. What the hell had happened tonight?

"Lugh." I rushed toward him and grabbed his hands. My fingers raced up his arms, across his chest, and up to his neck. I couldn't get enough of his skin beneath my hands. He was real and steady and strong, and I needed to feel every single part of him. I'd been terrified he'd never return.

He flicked his eyes up to meet my gaze. "My soul has been taken from this place. I can feel it. It's draining my energy."

I pressed my lips together. So that explained

the exhaustion. "I'm so sorry, Lugh. Let me get you to bed. I'll fill you in on the way there."

He didn't argue, another sign that he was not feeling himself. Otherwise, he'd probably be ordering me straight back to my healing ward bed. I slid beneath his shoulders, trying my best to support his weight, and helped shuffle him back to the palace.

On the way, he explained that he and the rest of the team had fought at least a hundred angry vamps while they'd searched for the fae in charge. And I told him what had happened when Quentin showed up. He didn't seem particularly surprised.

"We should have known he was going to find a way to get inside the castle," he huffed as we reached the door. I pushed it open, and we shuffled into the hallway. "There was always a plan behind the Sapphire scheme."

"You think he used the Sapphire to get us to seek out the sorcerer so that…what?"

"It was a trap," he said, sighing as we finally entered his room—with its millions of books. "He wanted me to go to Jezebel. Most likely, he didn't expect you would come, too. He must not have realised your strength as a warrior."

"Of course he didn't." I rolled my eyes.

Everyone underestimated me. "That said, we kind of underestimated him as well. I don't know about you, but I *really* didn't expect him to be teleporting around the castle."

Lugh frowned. "That is a very rare gift. And I don't doubt he'll use it again, for whatever he has planned."

We reached Lugh's bed, and I eased him onto the mattress. Only a few hours earlier, he'd been tending to me and not the other way around. My heart ached as I watched him close his eyes, settling onto the mound of pillows. It felt like I had a rock stuck in my throat.

"Lugh," I said quietly, reaching out a hand toward his face and then pulling it back. "I'm so sorry. If I hadn't answered that text message, I—"

"Then he would have gotten to the spear some other way," he drawled.

A snake squeezed my heart. "How? No one else inside this castle knows where you keep the spear."

"Uisnech knows. So does Saoirse." His eyes flicked open. "Please don't blame yourself for this, Moira. He was going to kill Uisnech. You didn't have a choice."

"But your soul…"

"Yes, my soul." He sighed and shut his eyes

once again. "Uisnech is the only reason I even have a soul. If it weren't for the goblin, I'd be lost in the nightmares. I'm glad you saved him. I wouldn't want him to sacrifice his life just to give me more time."

I sucked in a sharp breath at the resigned tone of his voice. He was so very tired, and he spoke as though he'd given up all hope. I'd never seen him like this before. Lugh was a lot of things, but a defeatist? Never. Not until this.

Not until I'd failed him.

"I could have stopped him some other way," I argued, balling my hands.

"And how would you have done that?" Eyes still shut, Lugh arched a brow. "He can teleport."

I narrowed my eyes. "I don't know why you're so calm about this. Quentin stole your spear. The very same fae who was working to bring Nemain back from the dead. You know what this means, right? He probably has the cauldron. He'll use the spear's magic to bring her back, and your soul will be gone forever."

"I have lived a very long life as Lugh." Sighing, he sat up in the bed, reached out, and wrapped his hands around my shoulders. His forehead pressed against mine, and Lugh breathed in deep, as if pulling my scent into his very soul—the one he still had, for now. "And I met my mate."

I shivered, curling toward him. I couldn't believe what I was hearing. Surely he hadn't given up. We could fight this. We could track down Quentin, fight him until he bled out on the ground before us. Find the spear and take it back.

"Lugh." Closing my eyes, I breathed him in and wrapped my hands around his. "Please don't talk like this. We're going to fight this. Together."

"Is it really so different than everything you've been saying all along?" He pulled back and searched my eyes. "You've been convinced that Caer's prophecy will come true, and the proof is before you in dazzling lights. This is our fate, Moira. You were right."

Frowning, I pulled away from him. "What are you talking about? This has nothing to do with Caer. If anything, it's the total opposite."

He gave me a sad smile. "When I lose my soul, I'll become the king of the *real* wraiths. I will have the power to unleash nightmares upon this world. That is why you will end up killing me, Moira. To protect the world. From me."

"No." I hissed the word as tears burned my eyes. Taking another step away from him, I shook my head hard.

"It makes sense," he said softly. "You would never kill me as long as I'm Lugh. The prophecy only adds up if I've become something else."

My hands ached from where I clenched them so tightly by my side. "I refuse to let that happen."

"Moira." He sighed. "I'm afraid we have no other choice. If I become what I fear the most, then I don't *want* you to spare me. I don't want to see this world destroyed, least of all by my own hand."

"Stop this." The tears began to fall now, hot and heavy onto my cheeks. "Stop talking like this. It isn't you. You're the king of the Court of Wraiths. Stand up and fight."

His eyes flickered with that spark I knew so well. "Tell me you'll stop me when I transform into a wraith, and I will speak of this no more."

"No!" I shouted the word and closed the distance between us. "I'm never going to kill you, Lugh. I don't care what you say. I don't care how much you beg. I'm not going to do it. You're not Angel, and I'm not Buffy. If you tear down this world, then I'm going down with you."

The words poured out of my mouth, heavy with fear, pain, and an intense energy that pulsed beneath my skin. Lugh stared up at me, exhaustion gone from his eyes. A heat had replaced it, and a ferocity that made my toes curl in my boots.

"You hate nightmare wraiths," he murmured.

My heart tripped. "But I love you."

As I gazed down at Lugh, a sudden realisation washed over me. The truth was on my tongue and hanging heavy in the air between us. All this time I'd been terrified that Caer's prophecy could come true. I'd thought up crazy scenarios to explain why I would suddenly turn my blade against my mate. I'd tried to imagine how I'd feel, what I'd do, how I'd act.

But there was one thing I'd missed. I hadn't taken into account my love for him. With the reality of the prophecy staring us down, I now knew that the prophecy had never stood a chance of coming true. I didn't need to go trekking through the snowy mountains of Faerie to find a "cure" for this. We didn't need to scour the ends of the earth for another druid who might have the answers. And we certainly didn't need to tap into the dark arts or any of the other magical solutions I'd considered over the years.

The truth was…I could never bring myself to end Lugh's life, nightmare wraith or not. I'd been running from him…for nothing.

"Lugh." I pressed my palm to his cheek. "I

should have stayed here with you instead of running. I feel like I wasted so much time."

That was the thing about being a fae. Sometimes you don't think about a week or a day or a month the same way a human would. We aren't immortal, but our lives are practically endless. There is always more time.

Until there isn't.

"Then don't waste any more of it." He growled and pulled me onto his lap, spreading open my thighs. I shuddered in response, a desperate desire ripping through my core. "We don't know how much more time we have left. Let's make the most of it."

A slight smile played at my lips as his hands began to trace lines up my back. "I thought you were exhausted."

"Oh, I was." He ripped my shirt over my head in one fluid motion. "But no amount of exhaustion will ever stop me from touching you."

His eyes flicked across my bare chest, and a delicious smile curled across his lips. He pulled his shirt over his head, and then yanked me toward him. I fell onto his chest, my breasts pressing against his strong pecs. An ache spread between my thighs, a need that I couldn't ignore any longer.

Reaching between us, I pushed down my panties and slid down his pants. He groaned as I slipped my fingers around his shaft, stroking the hard length of him. Fire danced in his eyes as I guided his pleasure toward the peak. I kept my gaze focused on his face. I wanted to see him when he fully lost control.

As his cock hardened even more, he growled and flipped me over, pinning my arms to the bed. He hung his head low, his tongue dancing along my neck. I squirmed against him, desperate to touch him even more.

"That's not fair," I whispered. "I was busy down there."

A wicked spark lit his eyes. "Not so fast. If we keep going like that, this will be over far too fast. I want to take my time with you. I want to be inside you when you scream."

I shuddered, arching toward him. I couldn't say I didn't feel the same.

His hands slipped down my waist, and his fingers gripped tight around my thighs. In a slow, exquisite torture, he pressed his length against my core. And then he dipped himself inside of me. He slid between my wetness, and sparks lit up in his eyes.

I gasped, my body shuddering from the length

of him. It was all I could do not to scream right there and then.

He tightened his grip on my hips, his fingers digging hard into my skin. His body rocked against mine. Lugh moaned as he hit the back of me, and I spread my thighs wider to curl my legs around his back. My entire body felt abuzz, the hot magic of our bond whirling through the room like a magnificent hurricane. I was barely in control, but I didn't care. I'd dreamed of this moment, I'd yearned for it. Being away from him had proven one important thing. I could run from him as fast as I could, but I would never escape how I felt.

I was in love with King Lugh.

This was it. Everything I wanted. Everything I *needed*. If I kept running, not only would I hurt myself, but I'd hurt him, too. I didn't know what the future would bring. Maybe one day we would come face-to-face with the prophecy. Maybe we wouldn't. All I knew was that I had to *try*.

We were in control of the future. Not some magical fate-like force that would guide my hand to do what I didn't want to do.

Lugh's eyes went soft as he gazed down at me. His lips found mine, and he kissed me fiercely, like he would never kiss me again. I sighed in his arms, moaning as he pulsed into me, again and again, guiding my pleasure to an almighty crescendo.

I clung on tight as the pleasure pulsed through me, as my body rocked with delicious spasms that shook through my core. He came only seconds later, his seed pouring into my body. We had come together, and this time, nothing could tear us apart.

Casting me a smug smile, Lugh eased his body off of mine and propped his head on the pillow. His eyes sparkled with a delicious wickedness I hoped he'd never lose. "So."

"So." I smiled.

"You sure you haven't been drugged with Sapphire?" he asked with a wink.

"I don't need Sapphire to want you."

"Does this mean you've changed your mind?" He arched his brow.

"About the prophecy?" I nodded. "I'm not going to let some random words from a druid control my future."

"It's about damn time," he said in a low growl, reaching out to pull me back to his chest again. Wow. He was ready for round two, and round one had only just ended. Fine with me!

Lugh suddenly gasped. His eyes went wide.

Arms falling limp to his sides, he stumbled out of the bed. Shock flickered across his face, his eyes lined in horror.

"Lugh." I rushed toward him, catching him just as he slumped against the wall. Eyes rolling back in his head, he fell, his muscular body ripping out of my grip. I dropped to his side, catching his head so that it didn't bounce against the hardwood floor.

I swallowed down my panic but shouted out the open window at the courtyard. "Help!"

I turned back to Lugh, cradling his head on my lap. My heart pounded so hard that I could barely think around the force of it. "Talk to me, Lugh. Come on, you're stronger than this."

Footsteps padded on the floor, and a twin pair of green toes edged into the corner of my vision. Uisnech let out a little gasp, and then moaned. "No, no, no."

Tears filled my eyes at the sorrow I heard in the hobgoblin's voice. "Uisnech, tell me what to do. No, wait. Call Axel, the sorcerer. And get all the healing nurses in here. Now."

A soft hand landed on my shoulder. "It is too late, my noble warrior. Lugh is gone."

"What?" I whipped my head toward Uisnech, my entire head full of swarming bees. "He's breathing. He's alive. We just need someone to get here and—"

"His soul is gone," the goblin whispered, his ears flicking. "You need to step away from him, my noble friend. The Lugh you know is no longer there."

Swallowing hard, I shook my head, staring down at my mate. His face was slack, but those sharp, cutting features of his still remained. Lugh wasn't gone. He couldn't be.

"I know you care for him, Moira, but he will not be himself when he comes to…." He skittered back on his oversized feet. "And you do not want to be quite so close to him when he opens his eyes."

At that very moment, those twin dark, soulful eyes suddenly stared right up at me. But instead of the fire, the warmth, and the intensity I knew so well, there was nothing. His gaze was empty and unseeing, as if I weren't there at all.

Then his grip tightened on my hands, so hard I swore my bones nearly cracked. And then he threw me across the room. My body slammed into the wall. Everything went black.

My head connected with the table. Again and again. It was the ultimate head-desk, and I never wanted to stop. If I did, the anguish lurking in the corners of my mind might rush in and drown me. Lugh was gone. Both literally and figuratively. Uisnech had filled me in when I'd woken, still sprawled on Lugh's floor.

After the king had come to, he'd thrown me away from him and then leapt out of the window, falling like Spiderman himself onto the cobblestones outside the palace. Then he'd disappeared into the night. Luckily, he hadn't attacked any of the fae inside of Castle Wraith, but that had come with a price.

He would be lurking in the streets of Edinburgh now—stalking the humans.

"What do we do?" I pulled myself upright and blearily glanced across the table where Saoirse was sitting, purple eyes wide and unblinking. All the colour had drained from her face, creating a stark contrast between her skin and her waist-length dark hair. Boudica, Warin, and Nero had joined us, along with Uisnech. We hadn't filled the rest of the castle in on what had happened—yet. We needed a plan first.

Not that a plan could make much of a difference now.

We were fucked.

"We need to recover the spear," Saoirse said in a low voice, her eyes still unblinking.

I perked up a little at that. "Have you seen a vision?"

"Not in such basic terms, no," she said slowly, and then frowned. "Lugh's future as a nightmare wraith is as muddled as the future I tried to see between you and him." Her eyes suddenly went sharp. "It's because they're linked."

My heart thumped. Of course they were linked. That didn't make me feel particularly better, though. I couldn't get Lugh's request out of my head. He wanted me to kill him when he turned into a nightmare wraith. He wanted me to fulfil Caer's prophecy.

"Before anyone suggests it, I'm not going to kill him."

Saoirse's eyes widened. "I would never suggest such a thing. He's our king, regardless of his current state."

Warin leaned forward, pounding a fist on the table. We all jumped, and Uisnech let out a little squeak. "Has no one else realised what this means? Yes, it's a bloody nightmare—pardon the pun—that Lugh's lost his soul. But this only happened because someone broke his spear. Or sacrificed it."

Mouth dry, I nodded. He was right. I'd been so overwhelmed with trying to keep my shit together about Lugh that I hadn't stopped to consider the cause.

Eyes wide, I cast my gaze around the table. "They've brought back Nemain."

Warin gave a slow and steady nod, his lips set into a grim line. "Yep, which means that recovering the spear isn't an option."

"Because the spear no longer exists," Uisnech said in a low moan, running his long fingers along the top of his skull. "Lugh is gone forever."

We all sat around the table, staring at each

other. I couldn't bring myself to speak. If I did, I knew I'd break down. I was barely keeping it together as it was. I had to focus on my anger and not on my sorrow. And not least of all, I couldn't let myself give up hope.

"Maybe not," I whispered. "He got his soul once. Surely he can get it again."

"It took deep and terrible magic, my honourable friend. That kind of magic does not exist in this world, not anymore." Uisnech sighed and shook his head. "As the years have passed, we have grown further and further from the creatures we once were. That dark magic, the deep, impossible kind that gave Lugh his soul...no one possesses such a gift anymore."

Blinking hard, I glanced at Saoirse.

She pressed her lips together. "He's right. It's dark magic that bound Lugh's soul to his body. The kind that druids possessed. No one practices that anymore. There are only a few of us left, and the newer generations never learned to tap into that kind of power."

"All power comes from the fae realm, right?" Boudica asked. "The portal is open. We can go back and figure it out."

"It's a nice thought." Saoirse gave a weak smile. "But it's a pointless trip unless we have someone who knows how to tap into that kind of power."

"Caer," I said. "She'll know."

"You tried to find Caer once," Nero pointed out. "And she refused to be found."

I sighed and dropped my head into my hands. "We just can't give up on him. There has to be something we can do."

"There might be one way we can bring him back."

I jerked up my head to find Uisnech crawling onto the table. He stood in the middle before us, his hands waving like windmills. "The cauldron! It has the power to raise the dead. We will find the cauldron, steal it, and use it to return Lugh's soul to his body."

My heart pulsed, with hope rather than fear. "You think the cauldron can really do that?"

"If it can breathe life into a rotting body, then it can certainly put a soul back into a living one," Boudica said, nodding.

Saoirse's wide and soulful eyes stared into mine. "The enemy has the cauldron."

A shiver went down my spine, even though all of us already knew that as the truth. "Then we will get it back from them."

"They will sense our objectives," she replied,

her lilting voice transforming into something else, something much darker. "They will know we are coming, and they will set a trap. To succeed, we must go left instead of right."

I frowned, watching as Saoirse's eyes cleared. She gave a quick shake of her head, sighing.

Arching a brow, I leaned toward her. "Was that a vision?"

She nodded, still looking a little dazed. "It came out of nowhere. I wasn't even trying that time."

"What did it mean, love?" Warin asked with a frown. "To succeed, we must go left instead of right?"

Saoirse shrugged. "Your guess is as good as mine. I only repeat what I can feel, hear, and see. Those were the words that came to me, but I don't know what they mean."

"Shit." I pushed up from the table and began pacing the length of the Great Hall, mind whirring. As thoughts came to me, I shouted them out, so that the crew could hear me from even across the room. "So they know we'll try to get the cauldron. That much is clear."

"They'll be expecting it," Uisnech added, his ears perking up. "They will try to outsmart us."

I held up a finger as I passed him. "Which

means we have to outsmart them instead. Quentin won't know that we know that he knows."

"Oh god," Boudica said with a laugh. "This conversation is starting to sound like that *Friends* episode."

"Where Chandler and Monica try to hide their relationship from everyone," Saoirse added with a grin.

Saoirse and Boudica exchanged a very enthusiastic high-five.

Brow arched, I continued. "Right. Now that we have this whole *Friends* thing settled, can we move back to Saoirse's prophecy? We need to figure out how to trick Quentin into thinking we're not going after the cauldron but also for real go after the cauldron. Any ideas? And please don't tell me we need to pivot."

Boudica and Saoirse grinned at each other, shouting simultaneously. "Pivot!"

Warin groaned and dropped his head into his hands.

"To be fair," Boudica said, "we're not far off the mark. Saoirse's prophecy said we should go left instead of right, which is pretty damn close to what I'd call pivoting."

"Pivot," I muttered to myself as I stalked

across the Great Hall once again. "How can we pivot?"

"Why don't we start with something easier?" Uisnech suggested. "What would the honourable warrior do if she wished to track down this cauldron?"

I narrowed my eyes. "I'd probably pay a visit to A Knight's End and demand that arsehole bartender tell me everything he knows about our mysterious nemesis. In fact, that sounds like a damn good idea."

"Which is why you can't do that," Warin added smoothly. "None of us can, regardless of how much we want to nail his balls to the wall. Anything else?"

"I would also probably be tempted to go back and question Jezebel. With my sword. She knew more than she let on. Of course, that's where we got attacked by vampires, so I'd be more cautious this time. Take some more backup. And more swords."

"I'm sensing a pattern," Boudica said with a smile. "Aggressive questioning techniques. Rushing in, swords blazing."

"It's my skill," I said with a shrug. "It's where I do my best work. Would you lot approach it a different way than that?"

They all looked at each other, murmuring slightly, and then finally agreed that yes—they were just as impulsive and aggressive as me. Even Saoirse. She might not go in swinging steel, but she'd happily put the bartender through some uncomfortable questioning.

"So if the aggressive tactic is out of the question, what do we do?" I asked.

Uisnech clapped his hands. "Nothing! You do nothing!"

We all looked at the goblin and frowned.

"While that will no doubt throw Quentin for a loop, I don't see how that will solve our massive, massive problem."

"He expects you to go on the attack. He will set a little trap and wait for you to rush toward the only contacts of his you know about. Instead, you rush toward Lugh."

"Rush toward Lugh?"

The goblin nodded vigorously. "Lugh will make some attacks on the humans. We need to stop him. He will also attempt to return to Faerie, to reunite with the nightmare wraiths. We also need to stop him from doing that."

"Trap Lugh first. Go left," I repeated after him. "And *then* go after the cauldron."

Warin had paled. "You want us to trap a nightmare wraith? That's impossible."

Uisnech grinned. "We will trap Lugh, yes. And then we will use him to draw the enemies out of their lair. Threaten whatever they are planning. They will want to destroy him themselves. And then and only then…we go get that spear."

$\mathcal{U}$isnech's plan was one hundred percent blooming mad, of course. The problem with trapping a nightmare wraith was… trapping a damn nightmare wraith. He would not go quietly into the night. He would not vanish without a fight. He would twist our minds upon us and put our thoughts through pure hell.

We wouldn't even remember why we were fighting him. The only thing we'd want would be to curl up into a ball and die.

And that was just if we approached him. If we did manage to trap him—against all odds—we'd then somehow have to cart him back to the castle and stash him somewhere far enough away from the rest of the fae, somewhere he couldn't escape from—and nightmare wraiths were strong as hell.

Otherwise, the Court would be full of endless screaming as he filled each and every fae's mind with horrors they had never even imagined.

Add the human element on top of that, and the whole thing was beyond impossible. It was impossible *times a million.*

Another understatement of the century.

So when I found myself standing in the middle of a bustling Old Town with my sword very visibly sheathed around my waist, I had to wonder if the little hobgoblin wasn't craftier than he seemed. Did he have some sort of mind-bending powers? Had he used them on me to convince me to go through with this whole thing? Because his plan was absolutely bonkers.

We'd all spread out through the streets, taking sections of the neighborhood to patrol alone, so that we could cover more ground in a single night (we needed to catch Lugh ASAP). Another check-mark in the Bad Idea column. Every horror film ever made was clear on one thing: never split up. And yet here I was, seeking out one of the most dangerous supernatural creatures in the world, all by myself. If Past Moira could only see me now, she'd give me a sharp kick up the arse.

A human woman bustled by, her eyes so wide that I swore they might pop out of her skull.

When I shifted toward her, she jumped. "Sorry." I held up my hands. "I just wanted to ask if you're okay. You look a little…spooked."

She wet her lips, her eyes flicking to my sword. "You're one of those fae." Her voice wobbled. "You live up there in that castle. You have powers, right?"

She looked like she might vomit on my boots, but at least she wasn't running away.

"Yes, but…you—"

She lurched toward me and dug her fingernails into my arms, and then she hissed, "There's something back there. And I think it's going to kill us all."

I opened my mouth to ask some more questions, but she pushed away from me and raced down the street. Slowly, I twisted my head to peer in the direction from whence she'd come. It was a small close, and the lamp posts had been knocked out. Shards of glass littered the ground.

My heart thumped hard against my ribs.

Time to break another horror film rule. I was going to walk into that dark, creepy alley alone.

With a deep breath, I squared my shoulders. Just up ahead, someone screamed. My heart tripped, and I picked up my pace, fearing what I would find waiting for me in the shadows. I had wrapped my head around the fact that Lugh—*my* Lugh—had once been a creature that haunted my worst nightmares. But it was a very different thing to know it and to see it for myself.

My feet left the main thoroughfare behind, and I stepped into the alley. Immediately, darkness hugged me tight. Flicking on my enhanced sight, I glanced around. At first glance, there was nothing particularly remarkable about this close. It was nondescript, practically identical to the dozens of other closes that wound through the city like a maze.

It stretched before me, disappearing into deeper darkness. Buildings loomed high on either side, and a few bins were pushed up against the walls. Windows from flats looked out from above, but only a few glowed from within. It was quiet and still.

Too quiet.

Another scream shot out of the dark.

It was coming from just ahead, right where that patch of shadows obscured the end of the close from view.

My hand found the hilt of my sword, and I pulled the weapon from its sheath. Holding it up before me, I inched toward the darkness, enhanced eyesight still turned up to max. If Lugh was lurking just ahead, watching and waiting for me to come into range of his nightmares, I wanted to spot him before he hit me with his power.

As I passed a bin on my left, I paused, narrowing my eyes at the view before me. The shadows twisted and turned, reminding me of Quentin's powers. Then before I could brace myself, Lugh loomed out of the dark. He had grown taller in the hours since I had last seen him. Or maybe it was just the pulsing darkness that surrounded him that made him seem larger than he truly was. His eyes were pure black as if his pupils had erased his irises. His black horns curled sharper and higher than ever before, twin blades cutting out of the top of his head.

He was fucking terrifying.

A human woman with bushy hair screamed and ran past me, barely giving me a second glance. Her feet pounded hard on the cobblestones, her arms pumping by her sides. The expression on her face gave me a sudden chill. Fear streaked through her wide eyes; all the colour had drained from her skin.

Lugh was on the attack. Not that I should be particularly surprised. We knew he'd go after people. It was just…my heart flickered seeing him in action like this. The Lugh I knew would never harm a human, not unless he'd been forced to protect his Court.

He strode after her, his eyes unblinking, his hands curled into pulsing fists by his sides. With a deep breath, I stepped in front of him to block his path. My sword was still raised before me, and a strange, eerie sensation flickered through me as the words of the prophecy rang in my ears.

"Lugh, stop," I called up at him. "It's me. Moira. You know, *your mate*. You don't need to attack anyone, okay? Just…take a minute to think about what you're doing."

I had no idea if a nightmare wraith could be reasoned with. Hell, I knew next to nothing about how their magic worked, what they felt, or who they were deep down inside. Based on what I knew, and everything about Lugh's spear, it seemed they were soulless. So trying to reason with him as if he were Lugh was pretty much pointless.

That didn't stop me, though.

Even now, like this, I viewed the terrifying wraith who towered before me as the male I loved.

"Get out of my way," he said in a low growl.

Okay, so he could talk. That was a good sign.

"Do you know who I am?" I kept my gaze focused on his face, searching for any sign of recognition. Only a blank slate answered.

"You are Moira. You are the mate of the male who once called himself Lugh, the fae who once resided in this body. Now step aside."

My heart pulsed. His words hurt far more than I cared to admit. It wasn't as if I'd expected his eyes to clear or for him to tweak my chin with his thumb before pulling me close to his chest. But I'd wanted it. Desperately. With every single bone in my tired body.

"So you're saying that Lugh is no longer with you," I said, more to stall than anything else. While we'd been talking, I'd pressed a tiny GPS device in my pocket, alerting the others that I'd found Lugh. They'd be here within moments. Together, we could trap Lugh and take him to the vaults beneath the castle.

A win-win situation, as far as I was concerned. Down in the dark tunnels, he wouldn't have the reach to cast his nightmarish powers on anyone, and he could take care of all those Sluagh in his boredom.

And we'd have in him our grasp when we finally found the cauldron.

It was the only hope we had, and I was clinging to the plan like it was my only lifeline.

To my surprise, the Wraith Lugh tipped his head back and laughed. But the sound was nothing at all like the real Lugh's laugh. When he really let down his walls, it was a booming, soothing sort of sound that felt like cosy winter nights spent curled up beside a roaring fire.

This, however, was pure ice down my spine.

"I remember everything that has happened, Moira Talmhach. Who you are, what we have done together, and what the male fae Lugh thought, said, did. All of it." Wraith Lugh sneered. "He wanted you to kill me, did he not? Why are you standing there speaking to me instead of fighting me as you should? Do you not wish to fulfil your prophecy? Do you not wish to rid yourself and this world of me? Or have you forgotten what I shall do now that I am free? The nightmare wraiths are coming, and I will make certain they will come for you first."

Tears filled my eyes, but I refused to let them fall. His words felt like a sharp stab to the gut, and the look on his face—one of revulsion—was one I was certain I would never forget. Lugh—my Lugh —would never look at me that way. Not even when I'd pretended to be a solitary fae when really I'd been spying on his Court. There had always been a wicked glint in his eye, a sparkle, a flash of his real self beneath the mask.

This Lugh, though…he was pure darkness. It was as if the very core of him had been cut out, only to be replaced by the shadows themselves.

His grin stretched wide. "Perhaps Lugh's time in my body was a gift. I don't even need to use my powers on you. All I need to do is speak a few words, and the horror is flickering in your eyes. Your pain is written all over your face."

"You wish you had that kind of power over me." A tear fell from my eyes, betraying me. Not that it mattered. This Lugh, even though he did not possess a soul, seemed capable of peering right into mine. Where the hell was my backup? They should have been here by now.

"Shall we fight then?" He took a step toward me, shadows rippling across his skin. "They say you are one of the very best sword wielders and that no fae can stand against you. But can you hold your own against a nightmare wraith?"

I swallowed hard, staring up at him. The last thing I wanted to do was fight Lugh. The wraith had done his level best to convince me that the male I knew had been a parasite, lurking inside his body until he'd been kicked out. But I couldn't believe it. Those pit black eyes were soulless, yes, but they were still Lugh. I had to believe that he was still in there, somewhere.

"I'm not going to fight you," I finally whispered, though I still kept my sword raised before me. Footsteps pounded on the ground behind me. "I'm going to trap you."

Lugh glanced behind me, his expression growing hard. When he spotted Boudica, Warin, and Nero charging into the close, he tipped back his head and roared. The sound thundered against the building walls that surrounded us, and tremors shook the ground. I stumbled back, my eyes wide at the intensity of his power. I'd been attacked by nightmare wraiths as a child, but I'd never seen them quite like this.

He was a hell of a lot more powerful than I'd thought.

"Idiots." He laughed, that eerie sound that scratched at my ears. "You think you can trap me? I am a nightmare wraith. Do you truly know nothing about what I am?"

"I know that we can't let you roam the Edinburgh streets, attacking innocent mortals." Boudica strode up to my side, her own sword in her hands. I hoped she didn't truly plan on using it.

"Where will you put me then?" Wraith Lugh twisted his gaze toward me and smiled. "In the castle? You think that hideous place could truly contain me?"

I glanced at Boudica. "Why wouldn't it?"

He let out that booming, terrifying laugh and shot his hands out by his sides. Instantly, shadows engulfed him, pulsing around his tall, muscular body like a shield. It reminded me of something I'd seen before—Quentin's power, his ability to vanish from one place and appear in another.

"Shit!" I dropped my sword and rushed forward, diving deep into the very shadows themselves, no longer fearing for my own safety.

My arms made contact with absolutely nothing. Instead, I tumbled forward, knees slamming hard into the stone ground.

Wraith Lugh had been right. We'd gone up against him while having no knowledge of his abilities or what his powers were. And as it turned out, they were far greater than we'd thought. Just like Quentin, he could vanish into the night. Trapping him was no longer an option.

## 15

"He won't go far." Warin charged forward to help me stand from where I'd splatted onto the cobblestones. My knees ached, but my whirling adrenaline helped dull the pain. "He's stalking the streets of Edinburgh for a reason."

"He'll want some energy." Saoirse stepped out of the shadows, joining the rest of us in a huddled circle at the end of the close. "It will be a long time since he has fed. He's hungry."

"Fed on fear you mean?" I asked.

She nodded. "Nightmare wraiths feed on fear, partially because they love the chaos it causes. But also because they need to feed to survive. Not feeding dulls his powers. He's going to want to refill himself before he does…whatever he plans on doing. Likely returning to Faerie to get the others."

"His powers didn't look so muted to me," I muttered.

"The shadow shifting?" Boudica asked. "Yeah, that was wild. Didn't you say that's what the Quentin wanker did when he got the spear?"

"Yeah." I frowned. That had been troubling me, too. Quentin hadn't just teleported. He'd shifted into shadows and disappeared. What were the odds that his power was the exact thing a nightmare wraith did? I'd learned a very long time ago that coincidences were *never* true coincidences, not in the supernatural world.

We all turned to Uisnech, who had been quietly twisting his hands together. "I did not realise that this was a nightmare wraith power. I thought only King Lugh could do such a thing, though I haven't seen him do it in decades. He said himself that it was a rare gift in fae."

"He meant *teleporting* was a rare gift in fae," Saoirse cut in. "He didn't see the shifting shadows himself or he would have made the connection. That's a nightmare wraith thing. Not a fae thing. When you teleport, you just pop in and out of places. Nightmare wraiths use shadows to move through the world."

My heart thumped. "But then that would mean Quentin is…"

"A nightmare wraith," Boudica finished, slamming her fist against the wall. "Dammit!"

I held up my hands. "Wait a minute. I met with Quentin. He seemed *nothing* like a nightmare wraith."

I'd always been able to identify supernaturals, by sight and by scent. Fae did not feel the same way that vampires felt. They certainly smelled nothing alike. Quentin had felt just like every other fae I'd come across. Besides, nightmare wraiths didn't just go around plotting coups. They charged through life causing chaos, feasting on terrified souls.

It didn't add up.

Saoirse's voice was hushed when she finally broke the silence. "I don't know what Quentin is, but he's more than what he seems. It makes me question his motives…his plans. We assumed he had the cauldron, and he was plotting to bring back Nemain. Perhaps we were wrong."

I frowned. "What do you mean? He was working with everyone else who was trying to bring back Nemain. What else would he want the spear for?"

"He wanted the same *thing* they did. Lugh's

spear." She let a beat pass without speaking. "But I believe they may have wanted it for different reasons."

Suddenly, the realisation crashed over me. Quentin, for whatever reason, did not care one lick about Nemain. He'd wanted Lugh's spear because it held his soul, not because of the powerful magic contained within it. The spear had not been a sacrifice to bring another being back from the dead.

"He wanted the nightmare wraith king," I murmured, my heart tripping in my chest. "He wanted to get rid of Lugh's soul."

Uisnech's mouth was wide as he stared up at me. "Oh my. I understand the plot now, far better than I ever have. Our nemesis means for Lugh to call the wraiths out of Faerie. That is why he wanted the spear. He wants to bring on the apocalypse."

~

It took a few minutes for that bombshell to sink in. On the one hand, whew! With everything going on, I hadn't allowed myself to ponder what it might mean with Nemain back in the land of the living. She had some serious firepower—she could predict what people were going to do next. It had made it next to impossible to take her down.

She'd start her crusades against the crown once again, desperate to rule over not only the entire supernatural world but the mortal one as well, transforming humans into indentured servants.

Luckily, it was becoming clear that we didn't need to worry about Nemain.

*Not* so luckily, the threat was far worse than she could ever be.

"Right." I ducked and grabbed my sword from the ground, shoving it back into the sheath strapped to my waist. "We obviously can't let this happen. Like Saoirse said, Lugh won't have gone far. He's still feeding. And we need to find him."

If we could manage to stop him from gathering his energy, we could stop him from heading straight to Faerie. The longer we distracted him from his goals, the more time we'd have to formulate a better plan than the one we'd originally had.

This time, we didn't split up. It would be the six of us against one nightmare wraith. Together, we broke out into a run and raced through the Edinburgh streets. Humans stopped and stared as we rushed past, but no one tried to slow us down. They knew about the fae who lived in the castle on the hill. They might not like us, but they also didn't want to get in our way. If we were rushing around like this, weapons clearly visible, shit must be going down.

My ears picked up another scream in the distance. Waving my arms in the direction of the sound, I led the crew down another close, this one more tightly-packed than the one before. Our footsteps slowed as we approached the darkening shadows ahead. Heart thumping once again, I drew my sword.

A tall figure curled over a ginger human who looked about eighteen. He had his arms flung over his eyes, his entire body squirming as the nightmare wraith drew the shadows from his skin. Strands of smoke drifted around the boy, twisting and turning like black ribbons of death.

"Lugh!" I shouted at the form. Suddenly, the smoky tendrils vanished into the night. The hunched figure stood, twisting toward our group. Wraith Lugh's dark eyes flashed with rage.

His lip curled as he sneered. "Your weapons are useless against me."

I twisted my palms around the hilt. "I thought you could remember all Lugh's memories. If that were the case, you'd know that underestimating me is one of the worst mistakes men can do."

"I am no man." He shook his head and laughed, a sound far stranger than the laugh I'd heard from him only moments before. The feeding was working. The nightmare wraith was coming to life with each and every poor innocent human he attacked. "No matter how many times you come for me, you will never win. For I can always do this."

Once again, he vanished into the pulsing shadows. The human leapt to his feet, cast us a terrified glance, and then raced out of the close and into the safety of the Royal Mile.

Saoirse let out a frustrated sigh and threw her hands in the air. "Lugh has a point. We're never going to trap him as long as he has those shadow shifting powers. Every time we find him, he'll just vanish again."

"Ah." Uisnech punched the air with his finger. "But the shadow shifting drains his power, his energy. As long as he uses it, he will need to feed more, trapping him here in Edinburgh until he's been able to have his fill."

I frowned. "That's great and everything—I mean, I guess we could spend the rest of the night chasing him around the city and forcing him to shadow shift—but the more he does it, the more he'll feed. The more humans he'll attack."

And the angrier he would get. Nightmare wraiths could feed without killing—just like vampires could. But also like vampires, they could easily lose control. Mortals could withstand a normal wraith attack, so long as the wraith wasn't intent on a kill. But if Lugh got frustrated and became far more brutal than he was now…the streets would be littered with bodies.

And it would be our fault.

I slid my sword back into the sheath. "This isn't going to work."

"We must stop him somehow," Uisnech argued. "My dear king gave me an order so very long ago. He insisted that I never allow him to return to Faerie if he ever lost his soul. I intend to keep that promise."

"Yes, but we need a different approach. Lugh's books," I said suddenly. "He's spent so much of his life combing through that library. Maybe he found something that can help us."

"If he had, don't you think he would have mentioned it to you?" Boudica asked with a frown.

"Maybe," I said. "Or maybe he overlooked something."

*There has to be some way to stop him. There has to be a way to get him back.*

"Uisnech," I said, cocking my head toward the hobgoblin. "How long will it take Lugh to gather enough strength to satiate his hunger?"

Uisnech tapped a long, green finger against his chin. "He will need more than one night. If he wishes to control the nightmare wraiths as he once did, he will need to build up his power. They have for so long resided in the fae realm. They may have forgotten him."

"So he won't return to Faerie right away," I said slowly before glancing to the druid. "Saoirse?"

She frowned, gazing distantly. "I cannot say. It feels as though the wraith wishes to return, but I do not sense a hurry in him. To go left, we must go right. It makes sense that we would return to the castle."

"Okay, return to the castle it is," I said, speaking with the kind of authority I did not have. In Lugh's absence, I had somehow become the de facto leader, even though I wasn't even a member of the Court.

A temporary absence, I reminded myself. Things were totally out of control, but they wouldn't be for long. We would find a way to stop the wraith from returning to Faerie, and we'd bring back Lugh's soul, all while taking down Quentin to prevent him from trying anything again. Oh, and stop his army of supernaturals. And whoever else wanted to kill us this time.

Yep. Just another normal night as a fae.

We grabbed the books from Lugh's room—or at least what we could manage to carry in a single trip—and piled into the library. I couldn't bear to hang out in his actual living space. There were too many reminders of the king there. Even his scent still hung in the air. Instead, we spread our books across the ancient oak tables and got to work.

It didn't take long for me to realise these books were bloody dry. One waxed poetic about the trade routes of the 1500s, going into extreme detail about what ports various ships used and the crops they contained.

I tossed that book quickly into the 'useless' pile.

Another talked about demon possession, going

into great detail about how a mix of blood and herbs was the only way to complete an exorcism. Next up was a book that covered the War of the Roses. That one was a lot more interesting, but again, it had nothing to do with nightmare wraiths.

Sighing, I glanced up and peered at my fellow comrades through bleary eyes. "Anyone find something useful?"

A few tired murmurs spread through the room. No one was having any luck. With a sigh, I turned to stare out the window, only to see pink streaking across a morning sky.

"All right." I shut the War of the Roses book and stood, stretching. "It's morning. Lugh won't attack when there's daylight. You lot should get some rest before we try again in a few hours."

Saoirse nodded, but Boudica raised a brow. "And what about you, Moira?"

I frowned. "I'm not tired."

"You look like you're about to collapse," Warin argued. "Have you even fully healed from that vampire attack you endured the other night?"

Nope. I hadn't. In fact, I hadn't even slept since I'd fled the healing ward.

"You should get some rest," Saoirse said, staring at me with her bottomless eyes.

In any other situation, I would agree with her. But I couldn't sleep. Not when Lugh was out there, wandering the streets alone. I was still convinced that he was somewhere hidden inside his body, trapped in a cage inside the wraith's mind. He needed me. I couldn't let him down.

"Fine," I said, lying through my teeth. "I'll go upstairs and take a power nap. Let's meet back here in three hours? That'll give everyone time to get some shut-eye and have some food."

An audible sigh went through the room, and soon, everyone had shuffled out of the library to return to their quarters for a bit. I edged toward the stairs, pretending like I would do the same. But as soon as Uisnech disappeared through the door, I raced to the window to watch them wander out of the courtyard.

Cracking open the door, I ran across the cobblestones and flung myself into the Royal Palace. Inside, I tripped down the hallway and back into Lugh's quarters. I stopped short as soon as I spotted his familiar sofa and the tiny kitchen only used for housing books. Tears sprang into my eyes, the horror of the situation landing on top of me in a sudden avalanche.

Sobbing, I sank to my knees. I could still smell him in here, I could feel his presence, almost as if he were in the room himself. His arms were around me, at least in my mind. Those wicked eyes flashed with pure desire.

How was I going to do this? I was just a warrior, good with steel. My answer to every problem I'd ever encountered in my life was to swing my blade at anyone who ever crossed me. To charge in with swords. To shove those blades deep into an enemy's skin.

It had always worked for me, too. Swordplay had always won.

Until now. I needed to beat the wraith controlling Lugh without killing him. I had to stop him from bringing the apocalypse down on this world, but I couldn't slice his neck.

Because if I killed the wraith, I'd kill Lugh.

And it all had to happen before it was too late. The clock was ticking on the time we had. Soon, Lugh would leave Edinburgh. Saoirse and Uisnech thought it would take a few days, but what if he went to Faerie tomorrow?

And beyond all that, I needed him back. The ache I felt was already too much to bear. Lugh was the other half of my soul, the half I'd never known was missing until now. I wanted him by my side. I wanted to wake up in his arms every day. I wanted to see that wicked smile of his curl across his lips.

I wanted him, in every way imaginable.

Fate was a cruel beast indeed. Just when I'd realised the truth of how I felt, he'd been taken from me.

Sobs slowing, I pushed myself from the floor and padded into his room. I cast my gaze around, my eyes falling on where an indentation of his head still creased his pillow. I climbed beneath the covers, snuggling into where he'd slept. With another sob, I breathed him in and imagined how it would feel to have his arms around me once again…

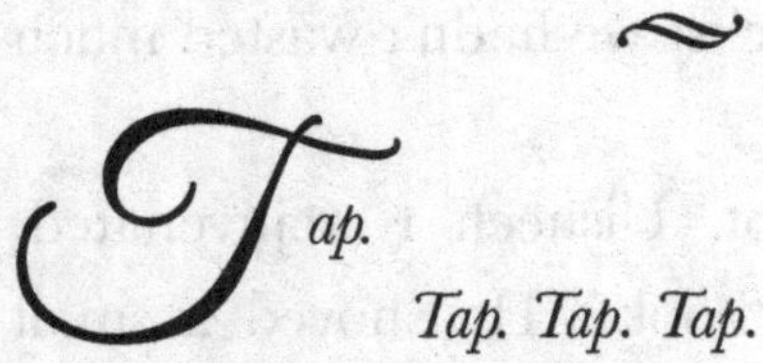

*Tap.*

*Tap. Tap. Tap.*

Something sharp and forceful knocked against my forehead, yanking me out of a dreamless sleep. I sucked in a sharp breath and sat up straight, my hands curling into fists.

Uisnech danced back and forth on the bed, his large ears flopping as he leapt. "The noble warrior has awakened from her slumber!"

Biting back a smile, I glanced around me. I

hadn't meant to sleep; I'd wanted to spend hours poring over Lugh's books. But I must have passed out sometime between crawling into his bed and snuggling into his pillows. I'd crashed hard.

"What's going on, Uisnech?" I rubbed my eyes and tried to find a clock, but Lugh didn't keep one in his room. "What time is it?"

"It is the best time!" he crowed, grinning.

"Someone has had too much coffee," I muttered, but I didn't feel irritated in the least. In fact, the hobgoblin's energy fuelled my own. I jumped out of bed and grabbed the first book I saw, ready to get started again. We needed to find a lead. And fast. I glanced outside. The sun was high in the sky, so at least we hadn't wasted much of the day.

"Uisnech has slept. Uisnech is rejuvenated. And Uisnech read a book." He shoved a small tome into my hands, his own fingers shaking with anticipation.

Brow arched, I flipped open the cover. The first page showed a drawing of the cauldron, and words in a language I couldn't translate had been scribbled next to it. "This is just the cauldron, Uisnech. We already know about this thing."

"You did not read the information." He snatched the book out of my hands and began to read aloud in a strange monotonous tone. "Every eye that sees this cauldron will be drawn to it. Every hand that touches it will desire to never let it go. Every soul—"

"Uisnech," I said, leaning toward him. "Cut to the chase. We don't have much time."

"Anyone who sees the cauldron will want to keep it for themselves, even if they are mortal and do not understand what it is." He snapped the book shut and grinned. "I have found our answer."

Maybe I needed to get dosed on the coffee myself because my brain wasn't keeping up with the conversation. "Explain, please."

"The cauldron vanished from Mary King's Close, yes? When the city began to rebuild it? Who was involved in that?"

I frowned. "Humans. The Mayor. Some workers for the local council."

"As soon as the humans found it, they would *not* have returned it to Lugh. They would have kept it for themselves." He shrugged. "I do not blame them for it. The magic of the cauldron is far too strong for a human to resist. It is also too strong for a nightmare wraith to resist."

My heart thumped. "Wait a minute. You're suggesting that a human got his hands on the cauldron, and that we could take it back and then dangle it in front of Lugh? Draw him away from Faerie?"

Uisnech grinned broadly. "Exactly, my noble friend. He will not be able to resist the call of it. We can draw him to us, and trap him."

Sighing, I shook my head. "But that still won't work. He can just shadow shift away."

"Not if we do it during the daytime, away from shadows." Uisnech's smile stretched wide. "And then we can use the cauldron to bring back his soul, before the shadows come again at night."

I jumped to my feet, pacing back and forth on the hardwood. Hope was a strange emotion. At times, it was as elusive as the wind. But now, so much charged through me that I could scarcely draw the air into my lungs.

"Uisnech." I stopped suddenly in front of the hobgoblin, grabbing his head and dropping a kiss on his forehead. "You're a genius. You've found a way to win it all."

"Brilliant!" Uisnech clapped with glee and then jumped off the bed. "We must start on our plan immediately! Boudica! Warin! We must gather the noble warriors at once!"

I nodded, getting caught up in his enthusiasm. "Where do we start?"

"Why, we must break into the Mayor's office, of course."

My smile died. Breaking into the Mayor's office was against every treaty we'd ever made with the humans. But we didn't have much of a choice. If Uisnech was right, the humans had the cauldron. This just might be the only way to save Lugh's life—and prevent the nightmare wraith from destroying the entire world.

## 17

This was the kind of thing I was supposed to consult Queen Clark about. Breaking the treaty with the humans had far greater consequences than just what happened here in Edinburgh. But we didn't have time for that, or to wait while she deliberated on our next move.

It was red tape that we just needed to charge right through.

We waited until nightfall. At this time of year, it came shortly after four. We left our strongest blades at the castle, choosing far more discreet weapons, just in case we were caught. A fae sneaking into the Mayor's office after dark was one thing, but lurking around with swords and spears was quite another.

The Mayor's office was situated in Old Town, just like most of the government buildings. It was an elaborate display of old world charm. The large stone building formed a square where an metal horse statue loomed in the center. Even in winter, wooden pots held colourful flowers, neatly manicured and cheerful.

A few lights still blazed in the windows. Someone was working late. If we had more time, I'd suggest we wait until close to midnight, but we couldn't afford to let Lugh fill up on human fear in the meantime.

Instead of sneaking in through the front, we found a door on the rear side of the building, backing up to a close that was barricaded by thick metal bars. We watched as some officers strolled through the area, took a look around, and then strode back toward the front of the building.

We all lurked awkwardly in the darkness, waiting for the on-duty officers to disappear around the bend.

"Wouldn't it be great if we had Lugh's mad teleporting skill?" I asked in a low voice. "We could just pop in and out, and this would all be over with."

Uisnech nodded sagely by my side. The hobgoblin had insisted he come along, even though he stuck out like a sore thumb. A massive green thumb.

"Boudica, what are you thinking?" I turned to the warrior, who frowned at the building as if it were her lifelong nemesis.

"They're going to have CCTV," she whispered back. "But also, why would the Mayor keep the cauldron here? Wouldn't it be better off hidden in his home?"

She had a point. Forget the fact that we had no idea if any of the workers had pilfered the cauldron themselves, there was no way to know where the Mayor had decided to keep the thing if he'd been the one to find it. A few hours ago, when we'd first come up with the plan, Uisnech's excitement had propelled me forward. Now the whole thing felt like a terrible idea.

"The noble warriors must trust me." His little ears twitched. "Hobgoblins know. It is in there."

"How do you know?" I asked.

"He's right," Saoirse answered instead. "I can feel a pull from that building, and the sensation that they don't want us to find what it is. A magical object. One imbued with great power."

"There'll still be CCTV all over the place, imbued magic spidey senses or not," Boudica muttered. "I don't see how we'll get in there without being spotted."

Squaring my shoulders, I stood from where we lurked in the bushes. "Just follow me."

Instead of booking it across the courtyard to enter the back door, I rounded the corner and ducked through the elaborate archway. The crew followed close behind, fanning out in a V formation. The officers glanced our way, but they didn't stop us. As long as you acted like you knew exactly what you were doing, and like you had little to hide, no one questioned you.

When we reached the front door of the building, I pushed inside, motioning for the others to follow me. As I shut the door behind us, I flicked my gaze around, lingering on each of the cameras mounted in the corners of the ceiling. There were two in the front lobby, at least that I could see. Likely, there were more that couldn't be spotted by a cursory glance.

A pair of glass double doors separated the entrance from a reception desk inside, a tall, gleaming mahogany structure where a black monitor hunkered on top. On the other side of the desk was another pair of double doors, also glass. But what lay behind was obscured by thick, closed blinds.

The crew stayed silent as I pushed through the first set of doors and came to a stop in front of the reception desk. A man sat behind it. He was young—early twenties, as far as I could tell—but his thinning hair was already turning white, and thick spectacles perched on the long bridge of his nose. He glanced up, a flush spreading across his freckled cheeks.

"Can I help you?" he asked in a nasally voice.

"Yes, we're here to pick up some files for an investigation into the supernatural activities of the local vampire gangs." I lifted my leather jacket, showing him the hilt of my golden dagger. "We work for King Lugh."

The man paled, and his eyes darted toward the double doors, where the officers stood outside. "Weapons are not allowed on these premises."

"By civilians," I said sharply. "I am not a civilian."

He nibbled on his bottom lip, his gaze returning to the edge of my jacket. "No offence, but what the hell are you, then?"

"I'm a fae," I said, speaking in a bored tone, acting as if this entire thing was some sort of routine activity I'd encountered one too many times already. "I work for King Lugh as an investigator. We have the same rank as a detective on the human police force."

He did not look convinced, but he didn't look as if he *knew* for certain that I was lying. "I've never heard anything of this."

Smiling, I pressed my hands firmly on top of the desk and leaned toward him. "Fae can't lie. Didn't you know? Of course you wouldn't have heard about this. It's far above your pay grade. Hell, I probably shouldn't have even told you. Keep it a secret, will you?"

He still looked uncertain. "I'll let you in, but you have to leave your weapons here at the desk."

I tried my best to look annoyed. "That is really out of the ordinary. You sure that's necessary?"

"No weapons allowed inside." He pointed to a sign that said that very thing. "I'll buzz you into a waiting room, and then I'll have someone come down to talk to you about those files. But I can't let you go in with your weapons."

Frowning, I glanced toward Boudica, who lifted her shoulder in a nonchalant shrug. "Bit annoying, but can't say I'm surprised. Last time I swung by, the other girl said the same thing. Forget her name. I think it was something pretty, something like…"

"Alyssa?"

"Yes, Alyssa!" Boudica nodded. "She wouldn't let me take in my weapon, either. Guess the policies are getter stricter. Not that I can blame you. It's tough out there right now. City's getting more dangerous every day. Which is why we want to help you lot stop these vampires."

I could have hugged her right then and there. Her words had softened the uncertainty on the man's face. Slowly, he stood and motioned for us to deposit our knives behind the desk. Once we'd dropped them off, he opened the next set of double doors.

"Just wait in here," he said. "The Mayor isn't here right now, but I can get someone else to come speak with you, who will be able to get you those files."

He shut the door, leaving us inside of a small waiting area with plush chairs, a television, and some generic magazines on tiny oak tables. As soon as the door had fully shut, I whirled toward Boudica.

"That was a very inspired speech you gave back there," I said with a grin.

She shrugged. "I took a page out of your book. Take a chance with your story. Sometimes, it'll pay off."

"And now we're inside," I said, rubbing my hands and glancing around. "Where's Uisnech?"

Boudica's frown matched my own. Warin and Saoirse had followed us into the waiting area, but the hobgoblin had vanished. I tried to think of the last time I was certain he was with us—about the time when we'd been hiding in some bushes. I'd been so focused on convincing the receptionist to let us inside the building that I hadn't noted if he'd followed us.

Closing my eyes, I sighed. "Please don't tell me he's running around causing chaos."

"He couldn't come inside," Saoirse said softly. "He's a hobgoblin. Most humans don't even know they exist. We never would have gotten inside if he'd shown his face."

"Well, then where did he go?"

She shrugged. "I think he might be scaling the walls."

Tension rippled through my body. If Uisnech got caught climbing into a window, the whole building would go on high alert. Any chance we had at getting inside the Mayor's office would go flying right out of the window from whence he'd come. I pinched the bridge of my nose, trying to tamp down my frustration. I loved the little guy, but I swore to the Morrigan, if he got us caught…

From the opposite side of the room, a door cracked open. Two large ears poked through, and then a set of yellow eyes followed. Uisnech grinned and waved. My stomach dropped into my boots. I glanced around, spying three more security cameras. We were probably being watched now, and the humans would have spotted a strange little creature scurrying around.

"Noble warriors," he hissed, motioning us toward him. "Come!"

Well, that was it, then. The jig was officially up. In a matter of moments, guards would stream into the room and haul us away. Whatever truce we had with the humans would vanish within an instant, all before we managed to get our hands on that cauldron.

So much for doing this the easy way.

"Come on," I said to the crew. "Might as well go with him and see what we can find before we get kicked out. The guards will barge in here at any minute."

Sprinting away from the doors, we joined Uisnech in the opposite hallway. He'd found a dimly lit corridor lined with closed office doors. Whoever worked in this section of the building had gone home for the night. That was just as well. Otherwise, they might get the fright of their lives.

"This way," Uisnech whispered. He half-jumped along the hallway, his floppy ears wagging with every step. The four of us rushed after him, stopping only long enough to swerve left into a second hallway. The lights in this section of the building were just as dim, but a glow emanated through the cracks of the door at the very end.

He pointed. "That is the Mayor's office."

I frowned. "Looks like someone is inside."

He nodded vigorously. "Yes, the great man is in there now."

"I'm not sure I'd call him a great man," Boudica muttered beneath her breath. "He stole the cauldron."

"The receptionist said he wasn't here," I pointed out. "Was he lying?"

The door cracked open at the end of the hall, and the Mayor's bulky frame filled the space. He had thinning hair on top and thick spectacles on his nose. "You mean my son, don't you? He is smarter than he appears."

I pursed my lips. Shit. No, *double* shit. We thought we'd conned the receptionist, when really, he'd conned us. "Mayor Richardson? I'm Moira Talmhach, and I work for Queen Clark

Cavanaugh, of the fae. I've also been working with King Lugh, the fae who holds court in the castle on the hill. We're here to speak with you about a very important matter."

He arched a bushy brow. "Yes. Some nonsense about vampire files. I'm afraid I can't help you."

Ah. So, he'd bought that part, at least.

"That's not really why we're here," I admitted, glancing around. "Could we come inside your office?"

"I'm supposed to trust a bunch of fae who sneaked inside with a fake story?" He laughed. "I didn't get to be Mayor by being gullible."

"It's important." I spread my arms wide. "And we're unarmed. Your son saw to that."

"I know the fae," he said, wagging his finger in the air. "You don't need weapons. You have powers of your own. We can speak out here in the hallway just fine, where my men have their eyes on you."

Frowning, I cocked my head and flicked on my enhanced hearing. Not far behind us, around the bend in the corridor, I could hear the unmistakable sound of hurried breathing. The guards had come already, and they were waiting to pounce if we made even the slightest wrong move.

"Fair enough," I said. "We're here to ask you

about an important fae object that was lost in the collapse of Mary King's Close. I believe King Lugh himself has spoken to you about it, asked your workers to keep an eye out."

He pursed his lips, his spine stiffening. "Yes, he did ask me about it, and we've told him all we know. The cauldron was never found when we cleared out the rubble. Wherever it was, it's gone now. If we happen to find anything during the rebuilding process, we'll send word."

I levelled my gaze at him. He seemed sincere enough, but there was a slight warble to his voice that I might not have heard if I didn't have my hearing up on max. "There's something you're not telling us."

He blinked. "You have no reason to doubt me."

"Except we have every reason to doubt." With a deep breath, I strode down the hallway toward the Mayor. Shuffling sounded behind me as his guards rounded the corner. "You see, the object we're looking for—the cauldron—has certain magical traits. Ones that make you desire to own it. If you found it, you wouldn't want to let it go. You wouldn't want to tell us it was in your possession because then that would mean it would leave your side. The cauldron was in that close, Mayor.

It didn't just vanish. Either you have it or one of your workers does. Either way, you know exactly where it is."

Bubbles of sweat broke out on his brow as he shifted in his shiny shoes. "Well, that's where you're wrong."

I narrowed my eyes. "Look, we don't want trouble. Just tell us where the damn cauldron is, and we'll be on our way."

"You're right. I did have it." He shook his head and laughed nervously. "I would have kept it away from you forever if I could have…that thing was…well, I don't know what, but it melted my mind. And…it didn't melt *only* mine." He glanced up, and his eyes went sharp. "Someone else has already been here for the cauldron. Some*thing* actually. Not a fae, nor a vampire, nor anything of the sort. Something full of shadows. It took the cauldron, and it vanished into the darkness."

**18**

We were promptly escorted outside, and we didn't cause a fuss. We'd found what we'd come looking for...kind of. The guards deposited us on the pavement just beyond the looming archway, giving us stern looks before returning to their posts.

I dusted off my jeans, frowning. "Lugh was here. He beat us to it."

"The biggest question I have is *why*?" Boudica asked, dropping back her head to stare up at the cloudy sky.

"Well, that book did say that everyone is drawn to the damn thing," Warin added. "He figured out where it was and went for it himself."

"They want it when they *see* it," I corrected. "When they're in the presence of the cauldron.

There must have been some other reason he decided to seek it out."

We all gazed around at each other, dumbfounded. I had no idea what Wraith Lugh wanted with that cauldron, but whatever it was, I knew it was trouble. And he'd just taken away the very thing that was the core of our strategy.

"Well, we can't stop there," Saoirse said softly. "If he's going after cauldrons instead of people, then he isn't as hungry as we anticipated. It won't be long before he gathers the other nightmare wraiths."

"We need to find that cauldron," I muttered, still grasping at the one thing that could bring Lugh back to me. Alive.

"If only one of us had a tracking power," Boudica said. "My fist fighting abilities have never felt useless before, but they sure do now."

I whipped up my head. "Tracking power."

"Yep." She sighed. "Unfortunately, I don't think I can beat the answer out of the ground with my fists. Might be fun to try though…"

"I know someone who can track," I said quickly. "Axel. The sorcerer. He helped me find Caer."

Uisnech chirped. "Axel is very powerful indeed, but he cannot track objects. Only people."

I arched a brow. "People like…Lugh?"

Uisnech's eyes caught fire. "And if we find Lugh, we find the cauldron. You are not only strong, my dear friend. You are clever, too!"

I shook my head and laughed, hope springing back to life. "Come on then. Let's go find us a sorcerer."

~

*A*xel lived in a squat little building that matched the rest of his street. The buildings were tall and thin, with mostly flats above the commercial properties. Some were pubs. Others were takeaway restaurants. There were even a couple of real estate agents on the block. Axel had gifted me with his address during our month-long hunt for Caer, just in case I ever needed his help.

For emergencies only, he'd told me. I was pretty sure this whole thing counted as an emergency.

I rang the doorbell for Flat 3, waiting on the stoop alone. The others had headed back to the castle to regroup, refresh, and check in with the rest of the guards. We were all running on fumes. Once we had a pinpoint on Lugh's location, we'd have to move fast. So the crew needed to get rest while they could.

The door opened a moment later, and Axel's scruffy face peered out at me. He wore a black t-shirt with matching jeans, barefoot. The skin around his eyes crinkled in surprise. "Moira? Didn't expect to see you here anytime soon."

"Gee." I grinned. "Nice to see you, too, Axel."

He grunted, waving me inside. "Don't take offence. You just caught me by surprise is all."

I trudged into the building, following Axel up a set of thin, carpeted stairs that looked as though they hadn't been cleaned in years. Dirt clung to the faded blue threads, and holes had been worn from the many shoes that had scuffed along it. He took me to the second floor, and then swung open the door to his flat.

The room inside was barren—or what the trendy called minimalistic. He had a single sofa in the very center of the room, facing a television set that squatted on the hardwood floor. A bed sat in the far corner beside the single window, white sheets rumpled as if he'd just rolled out of bed. Other than that…the place was empty.

"I see you like things cosy," I said.

He glanced around his empty space. "Too many objects messes with my magic. And to be honest, I'm not sure how much longer I'll live in Edinburgh. The city is cramped, dulling my senses. I do much better in wide open spaces."

"Makes sense," I said slowly. "Listen, there's something important I need to talk to you about."

He led me over to the sofa and motioned for me to join him. I sat, arse on the edge, too tense to relax into the cushions. "You still looking for that Caer of yours?"

"No. You were right. She doesn't want to be found, and I don't think she'd have answers for me even if I asked her."

He let out a low whistle, crossing his arms over his chest as he regarded me carefully. "Your tune has changed in such a wee time. Something happen?"

"I mean…where do I even start?" With a bitter laugh, I launched into the story of the past few days, careful not to leave even the smallest detail out. His expression ranged from incredulity to dread, and he alternated between leaning forward and sitting back every time my tale twisted yet again.

"This must be why you end up killing him." He shook his head. "Looks like the future caught up to you faster than you'd hoped."

"No." Voice firm, I narrowed my eyes. "I'm not killing him. That's not the answer."

Eyebrows winging upward, he frowned. "No offence, Moira, but it doesn't sound like you have much of a choice, unless you were exaggerating about his powers. The bloke is dangerous. You said so yourself. If he gets what he wants, this whole realm is fucked."

Tears burned my eyes. I wanted Axel to be wrong, but I knew he wasn't. In saving Lugh's life, I was sacrificing everyone else to a fate worse than death. "I'm not killing him."

Sighing, he shook his head. "Well, then someone else is going to have to. 'Cause he can't be let loose on this world. I know this whole thing is one big pile of shite, but you know I'm right."

"I know that I'm going to try to save him. And keep trying to save him, as long as I can," I whispered.

"Why'd you come here, Moira? It clearly wasn't for my advice."

"I need you to track him," I said, my voice still quiet. "I need you to find out where he is."

He grunted, crossing his arms over his chest. "So that you can what? Try to talk him out of it again? He's a nightmare wraith, love. He's no longer your Lugh. He doesn't understand reason, not like you and me. That male out there, feeding on fear, he's a shell. Lugh once lived inside that shell, but he's not there anymore. You've got to let him go."

"I'm not ready to give up. Not yet." I pushed up from the sofa, glaring down at the sorcerer. "Are you going to help me or not?"

Axel let out a heavy sigh. "Aye, I'll help. But on one condition."

"What's that?"

"You can try to do whatever it is you're planning to do. But if that doesn't work…you need to kill him."

~

*A*xel insisted I return to the castle to get some rest. He needed to gather some supplies for his tracking spell: he'd used up the rest of his herbs during our mission to Faerie. So he wouldn't have anything for me until the morning.

I hated returning to the castle empty-handed. I knew the crew would be waiting for me, hoping for information. Even after everything we'd tried, we still had next to nothing. Lugh was still out there somewhere, terrorising innocents. A part of me wanted to stay out in the city, racing through the streets, making sure he didn't harm anyone else. But I knew it would do far more harm than good at this point. He'd taken the cauldron somewhere. If we scared him off, he might leave with the cauldron, never to be seen again.

Until he returned with his army of nightmare wraiths.

Sighing, I trudged through the gates and into the palace. Checking the clock in the square, I found it was well past two in the morning. The entire Court was in bed, clueless about the madness going on outside these walls. We still hadn't told them what had happened to Lugh. Soon, they would begin to wonder. He hadn't been to any dinners in the Great Hall for days. Neither had any of the rest of us.

I'd never been a fan of keeping secrets like this. The fae of Castle Wraith deserved to know. If this plot to find Lugh didn't work, if we didn't track him down tomorrow, we'd tell them then.

Sighing, I drifted into the palace, not even thinking about where I was going. My guest room still technically lived on the first floor of the library. But I couldn't bear to sleep alone in there again. I ached for the comfort of Lugh's bed, desperate to sense him surrounding me, even if he wasn't there.

A tall figure blocked my route.

My sword was in my hands within seconds, without even thinking. Quentin's shadows pulsed around his form, twisting and turning like writhing snakes. He met my gaze and grinned.

"What the hell are you doing here?" I barked at him, edging closer, adrenaline buzzing away my exhaustion. "Haven't you done enough damage?"

"I'm here for the cauldron. What have you done with it?"

I blinked, confusion rippling through me. "What do you want with the cauldron? Haven't you already gotten everything you wanted?"

"Never you mind that. Just hand it over."

I narrowed my gaze. "First, tell me what you want with it. And then I'll hand it over."

He let out a chuckle. "Do you truly believe me to be that gormless? You only want to know my reasonings so that you can find some way to stop me from what I have planned."

"Fine," I said through gritted teeth. "You're right. Which is why you're an idiot to think I'd just hand the damn thing over to you."

Quentin stalked toward me, shadows rippling across his body. Frowning, I took him in. "What are you, anyway? I know you're not a normal fae. Not with that kind of power."

The wanker grinned. "A nightmare wraith bedded my mother a long, long time ago. I got the best of both worlds. Fae powers along with the shadow shifting of nightmare wraiths. It means I'm practically indestructible."

"We'll see about that," I said.

I lurched to the side, grabbing one of Lugh's swords off the rack he kept in the hallway. Quentin lifted his brow, grinning. "What happened to calmly handing over the cauldron, Moira?"

"You pissed me off," I snapped. "You want the damn thing? You're going to have to fight me to get it."

Lugh's words echoed in my ears. Quentin was not a fighter. He was a schemer. He might have nightmare wraith powers, but he had probably relied on them too much over the years. Based on his previous actions, the man had rarely handled a sword.

I had the advantage. And he knew it.

The shadows rippled again, and suddenly, he appeared behind me. I whirled to face him, sword raised.

"You seem strangely intent on keeping me away from the cauldron."

"Of course I am." I stalked toward him. "I

know what the cauldron does. And I doubt you plan to bring back someone like Florence Nightingale."

He disappeared into the shadows again, this time reappearing further down the hallway. Closer to the false wall that hid Lugh's den. Narrowing my eyes, I continued after him. Obviously, I didn't care if he went in there. It wasn't like I had the cauldron—but he didn't know that.

"I know all about the false wall," he said with a smile. "I already stole the spear from there once. Are you dumb enough to stash the cauldron there, too?"

He vanished before I had a chance to reply. An instant later, he stood before me again, frowning. "It appears not."

"*Obviously* not," I snapped. "And you'll never guess where we've hidden it this time. You want me to tell you? Fight. Defeat me. I'll whisper the answer with my dying breath. Or...is a nightmare wraith scared to take on a measly fae?"

That got him. Anger flared in his eyes. He turned toward the rack and grabbed a knightly arming sword, holding the short hilt with both hands. I bit back a smile. Everyone with even the slightest knowledge of blade weaponry would know that was a one-handed sword.

With a roar, I launched toward him. His eyes wide, he swung his blade at my head, blocking my blow. Our steel clashed together, singing in the dead of the night. The force of his blow threw me back, landing me flat on my arse.

Ouch.

Okay, so he might not know much about swords, but his strength was next level.

I jumped to my feet. Quentin pranced sideways, swinging his sword this way and that, like some kind of bizarre interpretive dance routine. Narrowing my eyes, I lunged. The fae laughed, the wicked sound curling around me as smoke filled the room.

Blinking, I stepped back. The damn wanker had vanished again.

~

*I*t took me awhile to calm down after that. I'd had my chance to take down our enemy, and I'd blown it. I'd waited for awhile, camping out in the hallway, hoping he'd return for another round of fighting. But he either must have given up or realised that I didn't have a clue where the cauldron had gone.

Either way, our fight was over. For now.

Sighing, I trailed into Lugh's quarters and propped the sword against the wall beside the bed, just in case. If I needed to awake suddenly, I wanted the weapon as close as possible.

Then I hauled myself into Lugh's bed and buried my face in his pillows. I wasn't sure I'd fall asleep. My mind whirred; fear clouded every corner of my thoughts. But the scent of him soothed me in a way that nothing else could.

Soon, I drifted to sleep, Lugh's scent curling around me like a cosy blanket. At first, my sleep was dreamless, my body weighed down by the exhaustion lurking in my bones. But soon, images sparked in my mind.

*I was in the forest. Somehow, I had lost sight of the route on the way home, even if I had made this trek a hundred times before this night. Winter had covered the lands like an icy blanket, dousing the light from the skies. The thick, grey clouds were endless, it seemed, and night came far quicker than it had in weeks past.*

*Shivering, I pulled my cloak tighter around my shoulders and glanced around. Imposing trees rose all around me. My footsteps in the snow were the only indication of where I'd been. Well, if I had made a wrong turn, then I had to retrace my steps. There was nothing to it.*

*Fortunately, I had my sword. If any deadly creatures lurched out of the darkness, I would be able to defeat them as only I could. My skill was in the blade. It was the only thought that kept me comforted this night.*

*Hurrying, I rushed back the way I'd come, my boots crunching into the deep snow. It had been years since the village had seen a snowfall quite like this one. It had put all the fae on edge. Whispers came with the heavy flakes. Rumours of monsters, of creatures that only came out during the deepest parts of the night.*

*As the daylight further slipped from the sky, I turned up my enhanced fae vision. Still, it was dark. In another hour, it would be far too dark for me to make my way home. I needed to hurry, or I'd be lost until morning. During the summer, there would be little to fear. But I could not survive alone in these icy woods.*

*My sword might protect me, but it would not keep me warm.*

*Somewhere up ahead, I heard the unmistakable sound of crunching snow. I slowed to a stop, cocking my head. Was someone else there? Had another gotten lost on the way home from the London markets?*

*A chill swept down my spine as the crunching amplified in my pointed fae ears. There were far more than just one set of footsteps. There were so many that the sound grew into an avalanche. Mouth dry, I held up my sword before me. It shook with my fear.*

*Out of the darkness rose dozens of dark figures. I could not see their faces, but I could feel the emptiness within them. My heart pounded hard as their scent filled my nose. They smelled of rot, of anger, of fear.*

*I had never seen these creatures before, but I knew what they were.*

*Nightmare wraiths.*

*Legends told of their existence. Dark creatures of even darker magic that feasted on the living souls. They came straight from the depths of Faerie's ancient caves, pouring horrendous nightmarish images into your head.*

*I stumbled back a step, glancing at my sword. It would do nothing against these creatures.*

*Heart racing, I spun on my heels and threw myself into the forest. Right or left, it did not matter. I just had to get away. Pumping my arms by my sides, I ran, faster than I'd ever run in my life. Still, the wraiths drew ever closer.*

*They were at my heels. I could feel their icy breaths on the back of my neck.*

*A hand gripped my ankle, and I fell face first onto the ground. Nightmares swarmed into my mind. Images of blood and bones, fire and screams, magic and tormented lives.*

*I screamed.*

## 19

"*I* have a hit."

They were the first words I heard, even before I peered out the window at the golden sun peeking over the horizon. The phone had jolted me awake, and I'd immediately slammed the cell against my ear, my heart clanging against my ribs.

It was Axel. He sounded weary, as if he'd been up all night. He probably had been.

I sat up straight, covers falling off my chest. "A hit on Lugh? You know where he is?"

"Yeah, it took some trying." He let out a shaky breath. "Lugh's not playing around. The magic surrounding him was dark as hell."

"Nevermind that. We'll take care of it." I sucked in a deep breath. "Where is he?"

"Craigmillar Castle. And I don't think he's alone."

~

Running through the halls of Castle Wraith, I gathered the sleepy crew. We formed a huddle in the training room, giving each other heavy slams on the backs and whispered words of encouragement. We all grabbed weapons. At least some of us did. Saoirse was going to stay behind, as much as a way to soothe the Court's nerves as a way to stay safe.

We all piled into cars and drove the mile to Craigmillar Castle. In the daytime, the site was much less foreboding than it had been in the dead of night with bloodthirsty vampires racing across the grounds. We parked a couple of blocks away and gathered at the edge of the tree-line, looking up at the crumbling stone walls.

"Right." I glanced at each of them in turn. Boudica, Warin, Nero, and Uisnech. Together, we had to make this work. "Us warriors will fight Lugh and draw him away from the cauldron, as long as it's in there. While we're busy distracting him, Uisnech will find said cauldron. It's daytime, so Lugh won't be able to use his shadow shifting powers against us. All we have to do is trap him."

"He might not be able to shift through shadows, but he's still strong as hell." Boudica nodded. "He will fight."

"Wounding him is fine." I closed my eyes at my words. I hated saying them, but I knew it would be impossible for everyone to get out of this unscathed. "If you can knock him out, all the better. Just don't…"

"We're not going to kill him," Warin interjected. "We haven't gone to all this trouble just to do that. If we wanted to take him down, we'd just go after him with as many swords as we have."

Instead, we'd come with staffs. Long, wooden poles meant to bruise, not to kill. It would be impossible to defeat him with such simple weapons, but that was kind of the point. We didn't want to defeat him. All we had to do was distract him long enough for Uisnech to work his magic.

I turned to the hobgoblin. "Are you sure you can do this? The cauldron needs a sacrifice. We don't have anything as powerful as Lugh's spear."

"There are some rituals I will try," he said with an eager nod. "I…I will do my best."

That was all we could ask for, really.

"Okay," I said with a nod. "Let's go. And make sure to stick with the group."

Quietly, we minced across the lawn and approached an archway that would lead into the depths of the castle ruins. I flicked on my enhanced fae hearing, hoping that we could hear Lugh way before we ever saw him. I didn't know much about nightmare wraiths. Did they sleep? If they did, now would be the perfect time to catch Wraith Lugh in the middle of some shut-eye.

We crept through the archway and found ourselves in a grassy courtyard. Green stretched out before us, leading to another set of castle walls, topped with battlements. The thick metal doors leading into the interior were still in place and shut tight for the evening.

Footsteps soft on the ground, we dashed toward the doors. One had been left open a crack. I glanced at Boudica and Warin, uneasy. Cracked doors that shouldn't be cracked were never good signs.

"Be ready for a fight," I whispered to the others before pushing against the metal door and craning my head around the edge of it.

No one was inside. Instead, we were only met by an ancient twisting tree whose leaves glowed green. We'd entered another square or courtyard of some sort, walls rising high on every side. The lower portions were mostly intact, though the upper floors rose in jagged peaks, roof nowhere to be seen. Rectangular holes stood empty, where the windows had once provided views.

"Um," Boudica said, pointing to a dark corner. "Axel was right. Lugh isn't alone."

We all turned in the direction she pointed. A blood-soaked body lay on the ground, limbs twisted beneath him. I winced and glanced away, bile rising in my throat. The dead man was Quentin. He must have come here looking for the cauldron, and...

Well, it was clear what had happened.

"Lugh's definitely here, then. Which way should we go?" I asked Uisnech.

He pointed at one of the open doorways. I let him lead the way, and we entered a room with a sign designating that it had once been the castle's kitchen. Along one wall sat a massive fireplace, large enough for ten men to stand inside.

Uisnech frowned. "This would have been quite a good spot for Lugh to hide, or for him to stash his cauldron. It provides some shelter from the rain, you see."

"I *was* in there. Unfortunately, this castle seems to have far too many visitors for my liking," a deep voice growled from the darkness. I whirled on my feet, my heart hammering. Lugh stood before us, a dark cloak obscuring his body and his face. He pulsed with power, shadows oozing from his skin.

I took a step back. "Lugh. We're just here to talk to you."

"Do not call me Lugh," he sneered, his hands curling into fists. "I am not that ridiculous male, and I never will be again."

"Okay." I shot a glance at Uisnech, who merely shrugged. "What shall we call you?"

"Nothing!" He shouted the word and stormed toward me. Out of the corner of my eye, I saw Warin nock his bow. It was the only true weapon we'd brought, just in case. "You are not welcome here. Get out. Get out before I eat every last drop of your soul."

I shivered, despite myself. His dark power washed over me, threatening to drown me in the depths of his nightmares. Shaking him off, I took a step back. "Calm down. We're not here to cause any trouble."

"Why else would you be here?"

I wet my lips, hoping his gaze would stay focused on me instead of the little hobgoblin now creeping out of the room so that he could search the castle. My role in this was merely to distract Lugh long enough for Uisnech to find the cauldron. With the other warriors surrounding me and adding to the distraction, we'd have our hands on the bloody cup before he even knew what had happened.

"Like I said, we just want to talk." I held up my hands in a display of surrender.

"Then why is this bloke pointing his arrowhead at me?" Lugh jerked his thumb at Warin.

"A very reasonable question," I said quickly. "He's just being protective. We weren't sure how you'd react to our presence in your...new home?"

Lugh scowled. "You think I would choose a crumbling castle for a home? The King of the Wraiths is owed far better than that."

"Oh, right. I guess you have somewhere better in mind?"

He pressed his lips tightly together. "Do not mistake me for a fool."

"Trust me. I'm definitely not doing that," I replied.

"I know why you're here." He stalked toward me, Warin's arrow following him with every step he took. "You want to trick me into confessing what it is I have planned. You think that if you know, you will be able to stop me."

"Maybe I will," I said, lifting my chin. "Like I said before, a lot of men have made the mistake of underestimating me. Go ahead and join the ranks of those, if you dare."

"And I said that I am not a man," Lugh spat, before whirling away from me.

Warin shot me a panicked look as Lugh left me standing in the middle of the ancient kitchen floor. He headed straight in the direction that Uisnech had disappeared.

Lugh's voice rose loud as he called out, "Oh, hobgoblin! Where did you go?"

"Shit," I muttered. "I don't think we were quite as stealthy as we thought we were."

My heart raced as Lugh disappeared through one of the many doorframes dotted along the wall. I followed him, pulling my long staff from the strap at my back. Uisnech had no idea that Lugh was on to him. The little hobgoblin could be pretty sneaky when he wanted to be, but he was no warrior. If Lugh attacked him...I didn't want to think about what would happen.

When I ducked through the door, I found nothing but another vacant room. Lugh was nowhere in sight. Fighting back a roar, I raced through the castle, poking my head through every door I found.

My fear grew with every step until I finally rounded the corner to find the hobgoblin gripping the stone wall, a grimace flickering across his green-tinted face. Frantic breaths puffed out of him.

"I'm okay." He held up a hand. "He gave me a good punch in the gut, but I'll live."

"Oh, Uisnech." I rushed toward the goblin, my heart squeezing tight. When I reached him, I threw my arms around him and pulled him close. "Thank the Morrigan you're okay."

"The cauldron is gone." Uisnech shuddered. "And so is Lugh."

I ground my teeth together, forcing down the bile that stung my throat. We'd been so close to stopping him. But we'd lost. And I didn't see how we would ever beat him now that he'd fled.

With a defeated sigh, I reached for my phone. "I'll call Axel and ask if he can pinpoint Lugh again."

"No need, my noble warrior." Uisnech's yellow eyes flickered. "I know where he will have gone. Back to Faerie. He's going to gather the nightmare wraiths. We have failed."

## 20

efeat was a bitter taste at the best of times, but it was far worse when it meant you'd lost the love of your life. Your soulmate, the one fae in the world bound to you by powerful magic. There was nothing quite like a mating bond. It was terrifying and wonderful all at once, so all-encompassing that it was impossible to remember a time when it didn't exist.

But beyond that, the loss of Lugh hit deeper than a mere bond. I'd never met anyone quite like him, someone who cared for the lost souls of the world, enough to start his own secret court to take care of them. I knew how he would feel if he could see himself now, hunting humans. And yet I couldn't give him the one thing he'd begged me to do: end the nightmares.

The rest of the crew had given up. Uisnech returned to the castle to alert Saoirse of the developments. She would plan a speech now, prepare herself for the news that she had to give the rest of the Court. They would be devastated.

Not as devastated as me.

But even after everything that had happened, I hadn't given up on Lugh. I never would. Not as long as I was still breathing. While the others crawled into their beds, I climbed into a car and sped out of Edinburgh, watching the city vanish into a small dot in the rearview mirror.

Terror tripped through my veins as I thought about what I was about to do. My biggest worry had always been that I would kill my mate, but the prophecy wasn't the only thing that scared me. Being attacked by nightmare wraiths as a child… I'd never been able to rid those monsters from my dreams. And now I was going to head straight into a den of them.

A den of very hungry wraiths, who hadn't fed in years.

It was the only way to save my mate.

The Lake of the Dragon's Mouth was hidden deep within the Devon forests, through a maze of twisting branches covered in deep green moss. Scents enveloped me as I made my trek up the hillside. Lilacs and wisteria. Moss and dirt. In the past, Caer had lived here in these dense woods, hiding the portal into Faerie from any wandering passersby. But she'd left, and now the portal was unprotected. Anyone could enter, so long as they knew how to find it.

Including Lugh.

I came to a tree-line and pushed through. Instantly, the landscape transformed before my very eyes. The damp chill was swept away by a bright, warm sun. Flowers danced in the light breeze, a kaleidoscope of bright, happy colours, the total opposite to how I felt deep down inside. Right now, I could use some bulging clouds and slashing rain, just so I could feel as miserable as possible.

I jogged down the slope of the hillside, aiming my feet toward the water. The ground looked disturbed, the grass flattened, as if something had passed by here very recently.

Lugh.

I picked up the pace and launched into the

lake before my fear could talk me out of my plan. Not that I had much of a plan, if I were being honest. At the moment, all I knew was that I had to get to Lugh. Somehow, I had to stop him from bringing the wraiths through the portal. Bonus if I could use the cauldron to get him back.

I swam through the dark waters, ignoring the dark pulsing that surrounded my body, warning me to turn back. Bright sparkling lights drifted by me, and strange swirls lit up the deep. Still, I pressed on, swimming until I was certain I could not go another moment longer without a breath. Until finally my face crested the waters.

With a deep breath, I climbed onto the bank of the lake. This side of the portal looked identical to the mortal realm. The only thing that gave it away was the light pulse in the air, the magic that caressed my skin.

The nightmare wraiths were rumoured to reside in a southern castle along a clifftop, not far from the portal. With the sun drying my hair and my clothes, I trekked through the forest, my feet smooshing in my boots from the damp.

It didn't take long for me to find it. Faerie was big, but the nightmare wraiths had chosen a home not too far from mortals. I came to a stop when I spotted the black spires scratching against the darkening sky. A few windows were lit from within, casting orange glows onto the ground outside. My heart twisted, along with my stomach. How many wraiths would I find inside that castle? And how long would I be able to hold my own against them?

If they decided to attack, I was done for. One wraith was bad enough, but a dozen? A hundred? More?

I shuddered just thinking about it.

But I had to save Lugh.

My feet slowed to a stop as I crossed the tree-line. The castle loomed large before me, blotting out the brilliant sky behind. A shiver went down my spine at the sight of it. The dark spires, the glittering steel windows. It looked like the home of terror. No wonder Lugh had chosen this as his home.

Lugh stood on the grassy courtyard, his long dark cloak rippling behind him in the wind. His gaze was hard; his body was tense. Behind him stood at least ten other wraiths, all bowed toward him.

"Moira." His strong voice drifted toward me, harsh and cold. "I suspect I should have seen this coming, but I admit, you have surprised me."

"I'm here for Lugh," I said, my own voice as clear and sharp as his.

He laughed. "Lugh is gone. He no longer resides in this body. You will never again see the king you love."

I fisted my hands, trembling. "Then prove it."

He cocked his head, regarding me carefully. "You wish for me to prove that I am not who I say I am?"

"No," I said with a dismissive wave of my hand. "I know you aren't Lugh right now. But you insist there's nothing left of him. I don't believe you. And I'm going to hound your steps for the rest of our very long lives unless you prove it. You want to be rid of me? Show me Lugh is gone."

A scowl rippled across his sharply cut face. "Or I could simply kill you and be done with it all. That sounds much easier, don't you think?"

Ice slipped down my spine, but I stood my ground. "I'm not the only stubborn one out there. You could kill me, sure. But someone else will come along to stop you."

"I'll kill them, too."

Instead of answering, I merely stared.

"Why have you come here, Moira?" he asked.

"I said that already" I replied. "I came here for my mate."

Wraith Lugh let out a low chuckle, shaking his head. "You truly believe you can save him. He's gone. He no longer exists. He was destroyed when I retook this form."

"Can you *really* destroy a soul?"

Wraith Lugh tsked. "What do you think it is that happens when one dies?"

"Well, that's easy." I crossed my arms over my chest. "The body dies. The soul lives on. Or are you forgetting that it's possible to bring life back from the dead? That's why you want the cauldron, isn't it? You're going to bring someone back."

A strange expression flickered across his face. "You know nothing."

"I know more than you think."

"Tell me then," he sneered. "If you know so much, then what is it that I plan to do with you, Moira? I certainly can't let you go, not after you followed me here."

"You can *try* to do whatever you like." I shrugged. "I'm not backing down, and I'm not running away. If I have to stand here on this lawn for a year, I will."

"I won't be here in a year, and you know it. I'm taking the wraiths back into the mortal realm, where they will feast for years."

That was what he said, but I didn't truly believe him. If he wanted to rush the mortals, then why hadn't he done that already? He'd hung around Edinburgh until we'd caught on to his hiding place, and now he was hiding out here. Nothing about the way he held himself suggested that he was in any hurry. In fact, he almost looked relaxed.

"We'll see," was all I said.

Lugh narrowed his eyes. He stalked across the lawn, coming to a stop only inches from my chest. With flickering dark eyes, he stared down at me. A strange light shone in one, but it was quickly doused by that impenetrable darkness. Power pulsed from his body, curling against my skin. It almost made me shudder in response, so familiar was the magic eking from his nightmare form.

"You think you can get to me like this," he whispered. "You think your words and your presence here can warp my mind, make me forget my mission."

Those were odd words. Why would Wraith Lugh be distracted by my presence. Unless...

"But you are forgetting who and what I truly am. A nightmare." He hissed the last word into my face, turned, and then stalked away, his cloak flapping in a sudden wind. "Be gone from here,

Moira. I will give you sixty seconds to begin your flee from this place. After that point..." He stopped to shoot a sharp glare over his shoulder. "I will send my nightmare wraiths to end you once and for all."

Lugh whirled and continued toward the castle. All I could do was stare after him, my heartbeat racing. Surely he didn't mean that. He couldn't be serious. Even Wraith Lugh wouldn't sic his nightmares on me...right?

But he would. Because as much as I sought out signs that my Lugh was still lurking inside that body, I knew he was gone. And now I had less than sixty seconds to get the hell out of here.

Clenching my jaw, I twisted toward the treeline. My feet sank into the soft ground as I threw myself forward. I didn't know how many wraiths Lugh had managed to round up here, but I had no intention of sticking around to find out.

I dodged the trees, my feet throwing up dirt as I sped into the forest. My enhanced ears flicked on, and I listened as the sound of a hundred footsteps charged through the forest behind me. Memories flooded my mind of a time so long ago. Decades had passed, but it felt as fresh as the day it had happened.

Wraiths stalking me. Wraiths pinning me to the ground.

I couldn't let that happen again.

Tears burned my eyes, blurring my vision. A stick rose out of the ground, seemingly from nowhere. It flew up and hit me square in the face. Pain lanced through my nose, blood spurting onto my lips.

I risked a glance over my shoulder. There were dozens of them. Black figures curved over, stalking through the darkness of the forest. They all wore identical black cloaks and hoods that obscured their faces from view. Monstrous creatures. Soulless. Hungry.

Hungry for me.

Fear was leaking out of me. I couldn't contain it, even though it was like candy for these creatures. I had to keep running.

Sucking in a deep breath, I pushed aside the pain and continued on. No matter how close they got, I just kept running. Arms pounding. Feet brushing the leaf-strewn ground. Eyes blurring from the tears pouring out of my eyes.

Eventually, I reached the next tree-line. But when I pushed through the bushes, I didn't see the Lake of the Dragon's Mouth rippling beneath the sun.

I saw...the castle.

Horror churning through my gut, I shook my head and stumbled back. Somehow, I had ended up exactly where I'd been. I'd gone in a circle. I hadn't escaped the wraiths. I'd run straight back into their path.

The wraiths flew out of the woods while even more formed a line blocking me from running toward the castle. I tried to count their number, but it was impossible. Fifty? A hundred? More? Enough to destroy the world, that much was certain.

And enough to kill me within seconds.

I held up my hands, scanning the crowd of hooded nightmares for Lugh. My heart still yearned for him, even after all of this. Maybe if he saw me, trapped like this, I could convince him to let me go. I had to believe that deep down inside, he did not wish to see me killed like this.

But he was nowhere to be seen. He'd ordered the wraiths to take me down and then had vanished into the castle. He didn't even care enough to watch. I was nothing to him.

He was right. My Lugh was gone.

Closing my eyes, I pictured his face in my mind. Soon, the nightmares would begin, and his face would transform into the beast who wanted nothing more than to see me destroyed. I wanted to remember him one last time, as the male he had been, the two of us against the world.

His face flickered in my mind. Wicked smile. Glint in his dark eyes. Warm hands caressing my body.

And then the nightmares began.

$\mathcal{I}$ awoke in darkness. The scent of iron and dirt pressed in close, hugging me as tightly as the shadows. I sucked in a sharp breath and reached a shaky hand toward anything I could find. My fingers curled around rusted metal bars, and I pulled myself to my feet.

I was alive. I could scarcely believe it. Lugh had attacked me. Or his nightmare wraiths had. Same thing, really.

The nightmares had engulfed me, drowning me. The last thing I remembered was screaming out his name. His face had flashed in my mind, over and over and over. He was Lugh, and then he was not, and then he was Lugh again. It was all I could think about as the bloody images had poured into my mind. And then darkness had pulled me under.

I should be dead.

Why had he spared me? Why had he thrown me...into some kind of dungeon? That was what I assumed this was. With the dirt and iron and flaking bars, it was the only thing that made sense. Instead of dumping me in a grave, he'd taken me as his prisoner.

In the distance, I heard the creak of a door opening. My pulse flickered in my neck, and I tightened my grip on the bars. Light splashed into the darkness, highlighting my surroundings for just a moment.

I'd been right. I was in a dungeon cell, looking out into a corridor that led to a row of more barred rooms. And I was alone.

The light vanished as the door slammed shut. Footsteps sounded on the floor, coming closer to where I stood shivering in my cage. As the intruder strode closer, the scent of him swirled into my nose. An intoxicating scent, one I would never forget.

I pressed my lips together, swallowing down the words. I wouldn't give him the satisfaction of speaking first.

"I see you're awake now," Wraith Lugh said in

that familiar growl of his. "You've been out for three days. You're lucky to have survived."

How *had* I survived? So many wraiths had descended upon me. The nightmares had driven me mad. Truth be told, I actually felt all right now, if a little weary. After an attack like that, I should be either dead or barely breathing.

"No thanks to you," I said. "You're the one who sent those wraiths after me."

"You're not dead, are you?" he snapped back in a sharp tone that matched mine. "I could have left you on the lawn to die."

That suggested he'd intervened, that he'd stopped the wraiths from ending my life. But that was impossible. He'd made that much clear. Lugh was gone, and this thing was a murderous wraith who wanted to see the end of the civilised world. He had no reason to save me.

"You know what? You have an excellent point," I said. "You were threatening me with death, and yet here I stand. You didn't let the wraiths kill me. Now why is that, Wraith Lugh? Or should I just call you Lugh?"

He scowled. "You are insufferable. I will truly never understand why the fae had so much interest in you. He should have killed you the second you stepped foot inside his castle."

"You're changing the subject," I pointed out. "I've noticed that you do that a lot. Probably because you don't want to answer my questions."

Laughing, he shook his head. "You truly think I spared you because of some deep hidden feelings leftover from the fae."

I arched a brow. "Do you have some other explanation? Because from where I'm standing, that's sure what it looks like."

Although I would have preferred if the hidden Lugh had also somehow found me better quarters than this. I didn't even have a bed, let alone a comfy duvet or some pillows.

And I didn't even want to think about the toilet situation.

"I have a far greater use for you," he said. "You will be bait for the others."

I tightened my grip on the bars. "What others? Saoirse? Uisnech? What do you want with them?"

"No," he growled, striding closer. It was still too dark to see much of him, but I could practically *feel* every outline of his body. The memories of his face were enough to make me recognise him amidst the shadows. "For the Morrigan. She is the only one who is any threat to my inevitable rule over the mortal realm. As soon as

I have led her here, the world will become mine."

*Oh.* My gut twisted. So that was why he'd spared me. Not because he found his feelings impossible to escape, something leftover from the magic of my mate bond with Lugh.

I was a muppet for hoping otherwise.

"Nice try. But that will never work," I snapped back, more for show than anything else. If I were being honest, his words had sent a sharp chill through my heart. He was right. The queen was our best hope for stopping Wraith Lugh's assault on the mortals. Without her, he'd barely have a fight.

I couldn't see his face, but I could *feel* the flash of his wicked grin.

"Ah, there you are wrong." He inched closer, dropping his voice into a hiss. "I have already sent her the threat. She is on her way, with a small ragtag band of fighters. She didn't have time to gather a large army. My plan will work, Moira. And you will have helped me do it."

Anger flashed through me, but the emotion was quickly replaced with remorse. He was right. If I hadn't been so intent on tracking him down, I wouldn't have delivered him the very thing that would draw the Morrigan out: me. I'd been so convinced that I could find the real Lugh hiding in the depths of the wraith that I'd risked it all. Not just my own life but the lives of everyone else.

"Ah." He chuckled. "I can see now that you have finally accepted the truth. I am not your Lugh. I never will be again. I have trapped you here to *destroy* you, not to save your life."

I wanted nothing more than to believe he didn't mean that, but there was no doubt in his voice. With my lips pressed firmly together, I watched him push away from the bars and head to the stairs.

"Good night, Moira." He threw the words over his shoulder. "Don't even think about fighting me. I have wraiths stationed all around the premises. The second you so much as look for an escape route, I'll have them attack you once again. And next time, I won't bother to keep you alive."

Lugh laughed and marched up the stairs. He pushed open the door and slammed it hard behind him, leaving me in total darkness.

With a sigh, I stumbled back and slumped against the dirt-stained wall. Tears filled my eyes and splashed down my cheeks. It was all over.

I'd lost.

I'd lost Lugh. I'd lost the fight against the

wraiths. I'd lost any hope I ever had of making it back to the mortal realm alive.

I'd lost it everything.

~

*H*ours went by. Or maybe days. It was impossible to keep track in the terrible darkness. My eyes had begun to adjust, but there was still only so much that I could see. The bars were thick and spaced only far enough apart for my fingers to slip through them. To my right sat an empty cell, where a blanket had been spread across the dirt-packed ground. Someone had once been kept there. I didn't want to think about where they were now.

Lugh came and went with surprising frequency. He brought me food, along with a bucket of crisp mineral water. Several times, I asked for a status about the queen. He never answered.

For all I knew, he'd already drawn her here, and she was dead.

But that wouldn't explain why he still kept me alive.

As long as I was still breathing, there was a

chance that humanity would survive the plague of nightmare wraiths...not that I had long.

At the end of the day—maybe, I couldn't be certain—Lugh brought down a third meal. He shuffled to a stop outside my cell door, eyeing me warily. Even though I hadn't made a single move to escape, he clearly didn't trust that I didn't plan on trying something.

"Back up to the wall," he ordered with a bored tone to his voice. "Make a move for the door, and I'll kill you on the spot."

I obeyed, lips pressed tightly together.

As soon as my back hit stone, Lugh swung open the door, slid the tray across the floor, and then slammed the bars shut again. The cell was locked before I could even take another breath.

I glanced down at the meal. You'd think prisoners would get gruel, right? Like some kind of disgusting porridge that was lukewarm. Instead, Lugh had brought me a veritable feast. Roast chicken, a pile of mashed potatoes slathered in butter, and some steamed vegetables. He'd even put a chunk of black pudding on the side, a dish that had become a favourite of mine at our nightly feasts in Edinburgh. My stomach grumbled in response.

He began to walk away, but I called out after him. "Any news on the Morrigan?"

"That is none of your concern," he snapped. "Eat your dinner."

Ah, so it *was* the end of the day. That was the first real tidbit of knowledge that I could mentally log. It didn't really tell me much, but I would take anything I could get. Nighttime meant shadows, which meant that Wraith Lugh was now at his strongest. In the morning, he'd be weaker. If my queen planned to attack, I hoped she'd wait until then.

Ignoring the food, I strode up to the bars and peered at his retreating back. "Can I ask you something?"

"You can," he said, pausing but not turning to face me. "But it is unlikely I will answer."

"Are all the wraiths like you?"

He craned his head, glancing over his shoulder. In the dark, I swore I could still see the hooded black of his eyes. "In what way?"

"You seem fairly intelligent. You have a strategic plan to take over the world," I said. "The other wraiths seem sort of...mindless."

"They are hungry. Until they feast on more fear, they will not be at full strength," he said in a gruff voice. "And they are not the king of the wraiths. I am."

I frowned out at him. "If they're hungry, why haven't you let them feed again?"

I didn't really want to give him any ideas, but any information I could weasel out of him would be information I could use later on. When I escaped. I was determined to get the hell out of here, even if it did seem impossible now. Sure, I didn't have a plan, but I had to start somewhere. First step: get the wraith king to talk.

"Sometimes, I think you have a death wish, Moira." He sounded so much like Lugh in that moment that a new wave of pain roiled within my heart. "The wraiths will feed once we take the mortal realm. Why are you asking me these questions?"

"It's boring down here," I replied. "I'll take any morsel of entertainment I can get."

Wraith Lugh whipped toward me and stalked up to the bars. Magic poured off his body, white hot and electric. Our mating bond snapped tight. I gasped, eyes widening in both fear and shock. The magic felt the same as it always had.

It felt like Lugh.

My heart shuddered, battering my ribs.

"Listen to me," he said in a low growl, leaning

so close that his face pressed against the bars. "I am only keeping you alive long enough to bring the queen here. Do not think I am showing you any kindness. Once I have defeated the crown, your life is forfeit."

He twisted away from the bars and stomped down the dark corridor. I stared after him, my heart hammering. He could deny it all he wanted, but I had felt the very depths of him just then. The wraith might have taken over the body, but Lugh *wasn't* fully gone.

He was in there somewhere. And I just had to get him out.

## 22

I barely slept that night. My mind whirred; my heart pounded in my chest. Wraith Lugh didn't want me to know that the real fae still lurked deep inside of him. He wanted me to believe that there was no hope. Truth was, my Lugh must have been more in control of his body and his mind than the wraith realised.

He'd kept me alive. He'd fed me three times a day. Good meals, too. Sure, that wasn't much. He'd also attacked me and locked me up in a cage. But a nightmare wraith would never have let me live, nor cared that I needed sustenance to survive.

Lugh was alive, and he was trying to take control of his body again.

When the door cracked open and footsteps pounded toward my cell the next morning, I was ready for him. Now that I knew the truth, I had a purpose. Now that I had seen the light in his eyes, I had hope.

"Back against the wall. Same deal as before," he said.

With a deep breath, I jogged back, holding my body tight.

Lugh cracked open the cell door, and that was when I pounced. I was taking a massive risk, but it might be the only chance I had. My body whirled toward his, my fists outstretched. Shock flashed across the wraith's face as I made contact, my knuckles pounding deep into his flesh. He stumbled back, leaving the cell door hanging wide open.

I rushed forward, my feet pounding against the stone floor. He roared as he jumped from where he'd fallen. I might be strong, but I knew the wraith was even stronger. I had to make it up those stairs and out the door before he caught me.

Fists pumping by my sides, I raced up the stairs and threw open the door. And found myself face-to-face with a dozen hungry wraiths. They stood, eyes glassy, around a sparse corridor lit only by flickering torchlight. A few glanced my way, but they didn't really seem to notice my presence.

*That's odd.*

No time to worry about that. Wraith Lugh had reached the steps and would erase the distance between us within seconds.

I had to get out of here.

As I rushed forward, I chose a random fork in the corridor, flinging myself left instead of right.

Lugh roared from behind me. I kept running, my feet pounding, my lungs aching, my arms churning the air—

My feet tripped on something, slamming hard into a random object strewn across the floor. With my hands flying up to catch me, I launched forward. My knees made contact with the stone, and a sharp stab of pain lanced through my body.

Dazed, I glanced behind me to see Lugh storming down the corridor. His eyes were wild with anger, and his entire body brimmed with that unmistakable power that was his. He bore down on me, his nostrils flaring.

I grabbed the object from the floor, jumped to my feet, and held it before me.

It was...

The five-pointed tip of Lugh's broken spear.

I stared at it, dumbfounded. "Where the hell did you get this?"

Narrowing his eyes, he stormed toward me. I jumped back several feet, pointing the weapon's five sharp points right at his chest. "Careful. The spear might be broken, but I can still use it to stab you in the gut."

Lugh went still, and his voice was dark and dangerous when he finally spoke. "I can call all those wraiths in here within an instant. You'll be dead before you can take your next breath."

I cocked my head. "Maybe. Or maybe you can just let me go."

Wraith Lugh might want to kill me, but the real Lugh would fight against that urge. It meant that I might have just enough time to get out of here alive. And save the rest of the world while I was at it.

"Hand it over," he said, his lips curling back into a snarl.

I arched my brow and lifted the spear just a tad higher. "You mean this old thing? Why would it even matter to you? It's broken."

"It is a powerful weapon," he countered.

Yeah, right. I could feel the spear just fine, and all the magic that had once resided within it was gone. It was still stabby, of course, but it no longer pulsed with power.

"It's dead. There's no magic here any longer."

He scowled. "A broken five-pointed spear is still a better weapon than one you'll ever wield."

I cocked my head and danced backward, waving the spear before me. "Last I checked, I *am* wielding it."

"Hand it over," he demanded.

"Why?" I shot back. "Tell me what you want with it."

He launched a hand toward me, but I was too quick on my feet. Darting to the side, I ducked low, out of his reach. He roared and rushed toward me. Heart racing, I whirled on my feet and ran. Up ahead, a door shone, daylight slipping through the cracks. All I had to do was get outside.

He was fast, but I was faster. I reached the door within an instant and pushed outside into the bright morning sun. The grass was soft beneath my feet as I raced across the lawn. I glanced around, getting my bearings. Hopefully, I could keep up my pace and make it back to the portal unscathed.

"Moira!" Lugh bellowed after me. "Stop! Give me the spear, or I'll kill your mate."

My feet faltered beneath me, and I slipped on the damp grass. Falling face-first toward the ground, I caught myself with the edge of the spear. Footsteps thundered toward me. I flipped onto my back and scrabbled away from Wraith Lugh, who stalked toward me with a deadly glint in his eye.

"I thought you said Lugh was already dead," I puffed, pushing up onto my feet. "You said he was gone. Forever."

"I lied," he sneered.

Wetting my lips, I took another step back and pointed the spear at his chest again. "Where is he? What have you done with him?"

"He lurks inside my mind." Wraith Lugh winced but continued his slow stalk toward me. "Quentin broke the spear, giving me control of the body. But still, Lugh remains inside. That's why I need the cauldron. As soon as the queen is destroyed, I will use it to fully exorcise Lugh from this form."

"How will the cauldron drive him out? I thought it was used to bring people back from the dead," I said, keeping him talking. I took another step back, stumbling a bit on a hidden tree root.

"The cauldron is a powerful object and can do far more than what you know. And it is the only thing strong enough to destroy Lugh completely. I intend to use it to melt the spear until it is nothing more than a sea of gold and silver. That should finally get him out of my head."

"Interesting." Another step back. "Unfortunately, I have no intention of giving you this half of the spear."

He matched my step with one of his own. "Put it down, Moira."

"What's wrong with those wraiths back there?" Another step back, and another step from Lugh. How long could I keep up this dance before he went on the attack? "They're just...standing around."

"It's daytime," he growled. "Wraiths can do little when the sun is in the sky."

Ah. Things were beginning to make a bit more sense now.

"But *you* don't seem to have any trouble at all with the sun." I darted back when Lugh took a swing at me. "In fact, you seem pretty lively to me."

Did that have anything to do with his connection to Lugh? Perhaps Lugh's existence inside of the wraith's body kept him a little more fae. He could walk in daylight, he had enhanced intelligence, and he had goals, plans, dreams.

"Are you sure you really want to get rid of Lugh?" I asked, pausing a moment in my retreat away from him. I'd reached the edge of the lawn. "If he's keeping you so...alert, maybe you'd be better off keeping him around for a long time."

The flicker in his soulless eyes told me everything I needed to know. Wraith Lugh had already considered this. He enjoyed the extra intelligence, the enhanced powers. With the fae inside of him, he was far stronger than he would be without.

"It is too big of a risk allowing him to live," he finally answered before narrowing his eyes. "Just as you have now proven that it is too big of a risk to allow *you* to live. I would have kept you safe for a time, Moira. Instead, you have forced my hand."

He launched toward me, catching me off guard. With a cry, I jumped back and swung the spear at his head. He knocked my blow aside as if it were nothing. I fell to the ground, teeth knocking together.

Wraith Lugh stormed toward me. I scrabbled back, grabbing the spear from where it had fallen to the ground.

As Lugh lurched closer, I jumped to my feet, whirling out of the way just as he threw his fists at my head. He stumbled forward, caught off guard by my movements.

I took that opportunity to throw all my weight behind the spear, jabbing it at his ribs.

But then I held my blow, stopping suddenly as the edge of the longest point brushed against his shirt. Heart beating hard, I stared up into his venomous face. Only a second longer, and I would have stabbed him right in the gut.

Tears burned my eyes as we stared each other down. I could still finish the blow. All it would take was another burst of fae strength, and the sharp points would sink deep into his skin. Caer's prophecy flashed in my mind. One day, I would kill my mate. This was the moment she had envisioned. She had seen us face off, and she had seen me sink the spear into Lugh's gut.

To save myself. To save my queen. And to save the world.

But I couldn't do it. He was Lugh. *My mate.* The other half of my soul. I couldn't stand here and watch the life drain out of his eyes, even if the wraith now controlled his body and his mind.

With a heavy sigh, I pulled back and let the spear fall to the ground by my feet. I had chosen my own damn fate this time. Fuck the prophecy, Lugh had always said. Well, if this wasn't a 'fuck you' to the prophecy, then I didn't know what was.

Surprise flickered in his eyes.

"Why didn't you kill me?" he asked gruffly. "You had your chance. You held back."

"Because while you might be willing to destroy the one you love, I'm not." I brushed aside the tears and stepped toward him, despite all the warning bells clanging in my mind. "If I kill you, then I kill my mate." I shook my head. "No matter what happens, I will never do that."

"Caer's prophecy," he murmured. "You are supposed to kill me."

Once again, intoxicating power pulsed between us. The mating bond.

"Lugh?" I cocked my head and reached out toward him. "Is that you? Can you hear me?"

Wraith Lugh suddenly snapped back into control and roared, his eyes flashing with rage. "Stop that!"

The two Lughs were clearly battling for dominance inside of the man who stood before me now. With a deep breath, I plucked the spear from the ground. I pointed it at him, my hands shaking.

"Give up," I said, inching closer. "I know you're fighting him. Give up!"

Wraith Lugh whipped his head toward me

and sneered. "Or you'll what? Stab me? You just proved you'd never do that."

He had a point. There had to be another way to get him out of Lugh's body. But how?

I glanced down at the spear. It all came back to this damn weapon. There was something about it. Something holding the fragments of Lugh together. Something keeping the wraith from fully taking control. The thing was...Lugh's soul wasn't inside the spear anymore. I could feel that it was gone. Instead, his soul was...

With a gasp, I looked up again. We'd been wrong about all of it. His soul had never truly been inside this weapon. It had been inside of his body, along with the wraith. They had existed side by side for decades. The only thing that had kept Lugh in control was the spear. Which meant, I didn't need to get Lugh back.

*I need to get the wraith out.*

Memories flashed through my mind. Pages of the books we'd searched when trying to find a way to defeat the wraiths. Nightmare wraiths weren't demons, but they were close enough.

"No," Wraith Lugh growled, his eyes going wide at the expression of understanding on my face. "Do not try it."

I took a step back, lifting the spear before me.

Gritting my teeth, I dug the sharpest, longest point of the weapon into my palm. A stinging pain lanced through my hand. Droplets of blood fell onto the grass by my feet, painting the green strands red.

"Stop it!" Wraith Lugh screamed, an inhuman sound that scraped against my eardrums.

I lifted my hand, curling it into a fist, and let the blood drip onto the sharp points of the spear. Wraith Lugh stumbled back, shaking his head. But then suddenly, his footsteps stopped. His body froze, his eyes going wide.

My heart hammered my ribs. Was that my Lugh, taking control of the wraith's body?

I couldn't wait to find out.

With a deep breath, I closed the distance between us. Lugh shuddered as I lifted the shirt away from his chest. Meeting his eyes, my lips twisted into a sad smile.

"I hope this works," I whispered.

And then I shoved the ends of the spear into his skin. Lugh screamed. I didn't push far, too afraid the weapon would slice him in half if I put too much strength behind this blow. I clenched my teeth, holding onto one of his arms while my blood mixed with his.

He roared and ripped out of my grip, stumbling away like I'd burned him with a torch. His entire body began to shudder, and his eyes rolled back into his head. I dropped the spear like it was a scorpion, fear and horror churning through me.

Lugh collapsed. His body went still.

Heart pounding, I rushed toward him and fell to my knees by his side. He wasn't breathing. His entire body had gone still.

Sobbing, I leaned over him and checked for a pulse. I didn't feel one.

Sorrow churning through me, I threw back my head and screamed.

What the hell had I done?

## 23

*L*ugh sucked in a sudden breath and lurched up from the ground. My hand flew to my chest, my heart restarting after what felt like years. He'd laid there like that for seemingly endless hours, his pulse gone, his breath still in his lungs.

"Lugh?" My hands found the ground, my fingernails digging deep into the dirt. "Is it you or is it the nightmare?"

His eyes flew open. A deep, deep black stared back at me, but not the dark pit that the wraith's eyes had been. Recognition flickered through his irises, chasing away the pain written on each and every line of his face. "Moira? Is...oh my god, are you okay?"

"What?"

He reached out and pressed his hand against my face, and then dropped his gaze to my hand. "You're crying and bleeding everywhere. What the hell happened to you?"

I glanced down at my hand, and pain suddenly blindsided me. He was right. Blood smeared across my palm as the wound bubbled with a fresh stream of it. The spear had cut deeper than I'd realised. I'd been so distracted by Lugh's collapse that I hadn't realised how badly I'd been hurt.

"Don't worry about me," I said sniffling. "Are you okay? Is the...is he gone?"

Lugh shook his head in confusion. "Is who gone?"

"You don't remember," I whispered.

"Remember what?" Lugh frowned, and then his eyes snagged on the weapon lying only inches away from his feet. Realisation dawned on his face, quickly followed by horror. He stared at the spear, and then jerked up his eyes to meet mine. "Blimey, Moira. Please tell me that what I think happened didn't really happen. Tell me it was all a terrible dream."

"A nightmare." Sighing, I collapsed back onto my heels. Finally, I could relax. It was all over. The terrible nightmare was done. Lugh was back.

He was here, safe and alive, and I would never let him be taken from me again. Instinctively, I reached out toward him, desperate to bury myself in his chest. I wanted him near me. This time, I wouldn't run. I would never let go.

"Moira?" Lugh's voice sounded tinny, and I realised my eyes were shut. "Moira. Talk to me. You're bleeding terribly. We have to close the wound.

Distantly, everything came rushing back to me. Everything I'd heard about lives and sacrifices. The cauldron and the spear. Nemain and Lugh's soul. It was all dark magic, the kind that took lives just as readily as it gave them. To save Lugh, I'd sacrificed my own blood.

And the magic would take it all.

Darkness surrounded me like a blanket, and a strange peace filled my soul. I wasn't ready to leave this world, but at least I didn't have to go alone. I had found my soulmate. And he had found me. Maybe in another life, we'd have more time than this.

My lips parted, and I breathed my last breath.

**24**

---

Of course, some endings are only the beginning. I, Moira Talmhach, had sacrificed myself to save my mate. It was only fitting, really. I had killed him, after all. It just turned out my blood had also brought him back.

And so *he* brought *me* back.

Bright light shone on my face, and my first thought was one of severe annoyance. My mouth was as dry as sandpaper, and my head felt as though it had been shoved into a blender. Every bone in my body ached. None of this was hyperbole. Whoever was bothering me with light needed a brisk punch in the face.

I cracked open my eyes and winced. "Am I in hell?"

Lugh chuckled.

*Lugh.*

My eyes flew open wider. He sat next to me on his bed inside his Royal Palace quarters, an ancient text open on his lap. I jolted even more awake. Lugh was alive and reading like we hadn't just been battling it out in the middle of Faerie two seconds ago.

And also, how was I even here? I had *died*...hadn't I?

"You are very much not in hell, Moira." He smiled and shifted to face me. "I'm glad to see you're awake. It's been far too long since I've seen your golden eyes."

"How long?" I tried to shift toward him myself, but ooooouch. No, thank you.

Doubt flickered in his eyes. "Don't panic."

"Why would I panic?" I asked slowly. "How long has it been, Lugh?"

Wincing, he shut his book. "About six months."

My mouth dropped open. *"Six months?!* How? Why? I don't understand what the hell is going on. Are you sure I'm alive?"

"You are very much alive." Lugh reached up and scratched the back of his head. "Trust me. I know better than anyone."

"What's that supposed to mean?" I whispered.

He didn't answer.

I shifted toward him, grabbing his hand and pulling it to my chest. He felt so solid, so real. But...different somehow. Hell, I felt different, too. Probably a side effect of, you know, dying.

"Tell me what's going on. You're starting to scare me."

He sucked in a deep breath and curled his fingers around mine. "It took awhile to determine what kind of sacrifice was required to bring you back."

"So I did die," I said, my heart pounding.

Slowly, Lugh nodded. "Whatever magic you tapped into to exorcise the wraith from my body...it was dark magic. It took your life."

Eyes widening, I stared up at him. "And you brought me back."

"We had the cauldron," he said. "But no idea how to use it. The books were fairly useless for a time."

"And yet..." I prompted. Lugh seemed so hesitant to explain what had happened. To put it mildly, I was beginning to get a bit nervous about the whole thing. What had he sacrificed? Another life? I wasn't sure I could live with myself if I knew someone had died just so that I could have another chance.

"The cauldron has strict requirements. There are few things powerful enough for it to accept. Life is, of course, one of them." Lugh's gaze went dark. "So I gave up mine."

"What?" I bolted upright, scanning his face, not understanding his words at all. "But you're sitting right in front of me, Lugh. I can feel your warm hands around mine."

"I gave it my spear," he said quietly. "The two broken bits of it. I thought it would steal my soul away, but I somehow survived."

I smiled. "It's because your soul was never in the spear, Lugh. You had it within you all this time. I realised that when the wraith couldn't rid himself of you completely."

And now, I was getting a second chance at life. A life with Lugh.

Lugh cleared his throat. Despite everything turning out all right, he still looked like someone carrying a heavy burden around his heart. "I suppose now that you're awake, you'll want to go our separate ways now. Your queen is worried about you. I'm sure she's eager to welcome you back home."

"You want me to go back to London," I said, frowning. The words sounded foreign to my ears.

He looked away. "Yes. If that is what you want."

"What *I* want? Of course that's not what I want." I shook my head and reached for his hand. "Is that what *you* want? I won't stay if you don't want me here, Lugh. But I want to stay with you. Always. You're all I want. It's why I fought so hard to save you."

It was the truth. Mating bond or not, I loved Lugh. I hadn't fallen for him *because* of the bond. I'd fallen for him in spite of it. All my life, I'd hoped I'd never find my mate. I'd outrun fate as long as I could, but it had finally caught up to me. And now, he was still here sitting in front of me. There were no more prophecies hanging over our heads. No more cauldrons or spears.

It was just us.

He looked back at me, surprised. "Of course I want you here. I just thought you'd want to leave, like you did before."

"Lugh." I leaned toward him and pressed my lips to his. "I'm never running away again. That I can promise you."

"Good," he murmured back. "Because you're all mine."

# EPILOGUE

The Great Hall had been transformed. The long wooden tables had been replaced by dozens of bow-accented seats. I stood in the center of the aisle, gazing forward as Celtic music swirled through the air. Lugh stood on the dais. He wore a black tux, fitted perfectly to enhance his well-muscled chest and arms. Warin, Nero, and Uisnech stood beside him. They all beamed at me.

As the music filled the expansive space, I moved down the aisle, my long white dress rustling around my heeled feet. I held a bouquet in my trembling hands, white peonies mixed in with splashes of golden roses.

To the left of Lugh stood Saoirse, Clark, and Boudica, all wearing matching golden gowns.

They all smiled, encouraging me forward, but I didn't need any help walking toward my mate. I did not have even a hint of cold feet. No fear lurked behind me like a wraith in the night. I felt happy, calm....free.

When I reached the end of the aisle, I smiled up at Lugh, who leaned forward to drop a kiss on my cheek. Today, I married my mate and the love of my life.

And I didn't need a druid's prophecy to know we would live happily ever after.

Wicked Oath

**Demons After Dark: Temptation**

Sinful Touch

Darkest Fate

Hellish Night

# ABOUT THE AUTHOR

Jenna Wolfhart spends her days dreaming up stories about swoony fae kings and rugged blacksmiths. When she's not writing, she loves to deadlift, rewatch Game of Thrones, and drink far too much coffee.

Born and raised in America, Jenna now lives in England with her husband and her two dogs.

www.jennawolfhart.com
jenna@jennawolfhart.com
tiktok.com/@jennawolfhart